GRETA GRACE

GRETA GRACE

by
Joanna Quinn

EMERALD LAKE
BOOKS
Sherman, Connecticut

Books published by Emerald Lake Books may be ordered through your favorite booksellers or by visiting emeraldlakebooks.com.

Library of Congress Cataloging-in-Publication Data

Names: Quinn, Joanna, 1967- author.
Title: Greta Grace / by Joanna Quinn.
Description: Sherman, Connecticut : Emerald Lake Books, [2021] | Audience: Grades 4-6. | Summary: Thirteen-year-old Greta Grace navigates the complexity of middle school relationships as she gets a new boyfriend, struggles with a bully, and has a falling out with her best friend.
Identifiers: LCCN 2021020898 (print) | LCCN 2021020899 (ebook) | ISBN 9781945847448 (paperback) | ISBN 9781945847455 (epub)
Subjects: CYAC: Bullying--Fiction. | Friendship--Fiction. | Dating (Social customs)--Fiction. | Middle schools--Fiction. | Schools--Fiction. | Christian life--Fiction.
Classification: LCC PZ7.1.Q555 Gr 2021 (print) | LCC PZ7.1.Q555 (ebook) | DDC [Fic]--dc23
LC record available at https://lccn.loc.gov/2021020898
LC ebook record available at https://lccn.loc.gov/2021020899

This one is for you, Tom, Morgan and Tommy.

Chapter 1

CANCER. YUP. *That's exactly what Casey Cunningham is like. Just like the poisonous, hateful disease that riddled its way through my grandmother's body. She's toxic. Hateful. I'm not lying. She is.*

"Greta Grace, is it true?" Samantha frantically grabbed me by the sleeve of my shirt, which, by the way, I spent a lot of time picking out. "Sarah said that Casey was glaring at you and made a comment when Mrs. Barrett handed back your science test. Is that true?"

"Yeah, but it's not my fault she got a D." I threw the shredded straps of my backpack over my shoulder and started down the hall, with Samantha walking quickly beside me. "I mean, seriously. She's mad because I did good on a test? That's just so stupid."

"Okay, but do you remember how she tortured Emily last year? Remember, she 'accidentally' slammed her into the wall. She 'accidentally' spilled neon-green paint all over her new boots, and she 'accidentally' made her face-plant in front of everyone at the chorus concert. And do you remember she managed to not get caught, not even once, and do you remember how she would post something humiliating online every morning? Even though Casey never used Emily's name, everyone knew who she was talking about. Remember?"

"I know, but, like, what am I supposed to do?" I looked at Samantha to see if she had an answer to this impossible question. She was making me nervous! "For now, though," I said, "we're going to get on the bus and forget that that too-tall beast with red hair and brown hawk-like eyes even exists. We'll show her we don't even care."

Samantha looked at me with a scrunched-up, not-so-sure kind of face and said, "That's what we are going to do?"

"Yep. That's what we are going to do." I sighed and climbed onto the bus.

"Greta Grace! Oh, Greta Grace. Come sit here, Greta Grace!" From the back of the bus, the red-haired vulture sang my name out over and over in her deep, scruffy voice. I hated her. I walked past Charlie Tierney, and he didn't even look up, but I didn't care.

My moment of confidence disappeared. I knew I was in rough shape when I didn't even care if Charlie noticed me. Then again, why would he when he hadn't the other 1,888,222 times I was on the bus with him? Even if he did, I bet the same thing would happen that happened in fifth grade when I liked Kyle McKelly. As soon as he found out I liked him, he went from picking me first for every team in gym class to leaving me to the other team to pick, usually last. It was awful. *Wait! Why was I even thinking of this?*

I needed to focus on Casey Cunningham right now. I sat in my seat, closed my eyes, took some slow deep breaths, and prayed to my angels that she would just shut up, but she didn't.

"Finally, our stop," Samantha whispered. We looked straight ahead so there wouldn't be any eye contact with Casey and then got off the bus and watched it drive away.

"If only that bus would keep going until it drove Casey Cunningham right off this planet." Samantha looked at me to see if I was still paying attention. "Don't you think it's weird that sometimes she gets off before us, sometimes after us, and that she's barely ever on the bus in the mornings?"

"I don't know, but it doesn't really matter. I'm sure she's here to stay." I sighed.

Samantha put her hand up for our daily departing personal handshake: high five, shoulder nudge, clap twice, and a hug. "I'll call you after my piano lesson, but don't worry. We'll figure this out."

Chapter 2

AS I SLOWLY ROUNDED THE CORNER to Mrs. McGee's house, I could see her kneeling in her front yard with potted plants and her spade. Brushing a bead of sweat off her upper lip, she stood up, took off her pink floppy sun hat, and pulled her white curls into place.

"Hello, my sweet girl. How was your day?" She peeled her flowered gardening gloves off and rubbed her hands together. "Gardening is not as easy anymore with these arthritic fingers, Greta Grace, but these arms are still good for giving hugs."

She always hugged me like she hadn't seen me in a week, even though I saw her every day. In fact, I bet that I've seen her practically every day since I was five years old, and I'm not even exaggerating. That was when Dad left, after he announced that he "just couldn't do this anymore." I still remember it perfectly. I'm pretty sure I was the "this" he couldn't do anymore.

Mom was so sad back then, so she and I spent tons of time at Mrs. McGee's house. They would talk while I drew and colored pictures and played with Rudy, Mrs. McGee's adorable, white fluffy dog. That was when Mom got all spiritual and stuff. Dad sent birthday cards for a couple of years, and then he disappeared. Maybe he's dead. I don't really care, but Mom insisted I talk to someone about it, so I went and talked to a therapist. He was super nice, but he just kept telling me the same thing Mom told me. "This has nothing to do with you. He has his own issues. Blah, blah, blah…" Whatever. I'm over it. We don't need him anyway.

"Greta Grace, are you okay, sweetie? You seem like you are in another world."

I pouted. "I was just about to tell you about how awful my day was, Mrs. McGee. Like, for real. It was the worst ever." I tossed my backpack on the steps and grabbed my gardening gloves off the white iron bench. They were a perfect match to the ones Mrs. McGee had, but much smaller. Everything about me is small. Mom said I am due for a big growth spurt but to remember that "good things come in small packages." Not sure what that means.

The one good thing about being small is that I'm the fastest one on our lacrosse team. Looks like I still am this year too. The coach said that's because I'm so close to the ground. I wonder if that's true?

Anyway, everybody knows that if Casey Cunningham starts calling out your name on the bus, you're in trouble. Big trouble. Her words are worse than paint tossed on you or something crazy like that.

She embarrasses people so badly. She'll make fun of anything—zits, weight, clothes and even your mother. So now, if she walks into the cafeteria and doesn't have a seat at the lunch table she sits at, two or three girls will get up and offer her their chairs. If she doesn't have a pencil in class, whatever girl sits closest to her will give her one. I think even the boys are scared of her.

Maybe it's all for show, though. Once, I caught her being nice to some of the little kids in the elementary school right next to our school, but she had no idea I saw. If she did, she probably would have knocked them down or something.

Chapter 3

Ms. McGee moved a couple of plants off the walk and set down her spade. "Well, let me get us some lemonade and a treat, and we'll figure this out for you."

"No, I'll get it." I kicked my backpack off the step, dusting it off for her to sit down on.

Flowers from her garden sat in a pretty blue vase on her sparkling glass kitchen table, and classical music played softly in the background. A book, *The Spiritual Laws of Daily Living*, was on the counter, opened up to her lesson for the day. I read the title quickly. "In stillness lies all the answers." She had read that one to me many times.

I pulled out the round sunflower tray, poured two glasses of lemonade, and got two chocolate mint cookies for me and two for her.

With the tray in my hands, I started toward the door. Mrs. McGee was usually really good at fixing problems. Maybe she could do it again. I sure hoped so.

"Mrs. McGee, your phone is ringing!" I yelled louder and walked faster. Shoot! "Mrs. McGee!"

But the answering machine got there first. "Hello. You have reached Molly McGee and Rudy. Please leave a message after the beep."

"Hello, Molly. This is Dr. Klyne's office. We need to speak with you. Please call us at your earliest convenience."

I just about stumbled over Rudy, who had followed me in, and put the tray down on Mrs. McGee's hall table to think for a minute. Dr. Klyne. He's the cancer doctor that Grandma went to. I know that was his name because I remember seeing it on the door to his office every time I went with Mom and Grandma. Why was he calling Mrs. McGee? Why would she need to call at her earliest convenience?

My stomach was queasy, and my brain was in a fog. I picked up the tray and started to walk out, but turned around and put the tray back down. That was just like the phone call Grandma got when she found out she was sick. I told myself to stop thinking crazy thoughts, picked up the tray, and headed outside.

"Thank you, Greta Grace. Nothing like a frosty glass of lemonade on a warm day like today with my favorite girl." She took a big sip from her glass, as if it were the best drink she ever had. My heart was pounding and my legs were shaking. I sat next to her on the step. *Why the heck was Dr. Klyne calling Mrs. McGee?*

"Now, tell me what was so awful today." She scooted closer and took a bite of her cookie.

I decided to lie. I figured God would understand, under the circumstances. She might have her own problem to deal with. She didn't need mine as well. "It's my math class," I told her. "It's just so hard."

I put on my best smile and looked at my sneakers. Mrs. McGee tugged on the ends of my hair and brushed some strays away from my eyes. "Are you sure? It sounded like it was something more than that."

"Yeah, I'm sure." My heart sank. Mrs. McGee just got a call from Dr. Klyne, and my only chance at solving my problem was slipping right through my fingers. I tried to fake being okay.

I pointed to the two huge bushes of pink and white roses lined up along her white painted fence. "Our roses look great, huh?"

"Yes, they do, Greta Grace. No, Rudy, you naughty dog. Out of my flowers." She scooped up the dog to sit on her lap.

"I have a ton of homework, so I better go, Mrs. McGee, and it's Thursday, so you have to go to Elizabeth's for tea."

"Yes, and we know how worried my dear friend gets if I am late." She squeezed my cheeks, kissed me on the forehead, and let out a laugh.

"Uh. But first, Mrs. McGee..." *Should I warn her about the message?* "I'll see you tomorrow," I said instead, clutched my backpack, and headed slowly toward her gate. I stopped and turned back, but I just waved.

I could hear Mom's voice saying, "You can say anything you have to say to anybody as long as it comes from a place of love." But I couldn't. There didn't seem anything loving about telling someone they got a call from Dr. Klyne.

Waving goodbye, Mrs. McGee stood up, tucked Rudy under her arm, and opened the screen door. I watched her disappear into the house. The door shut.

"Oh, my gosh," I muttered. "She's about to get that message. I should have warned her."

Chapter 4

"GRETA GRACE, SAMANTHA IS HERE." Mom yelled up the stairs.

I jumped out of bed, splashed cold water on my face because I didn't have time to warm it up, brushed my teeth, and threw on the first outfit I got my hands on: a pair of jean shorts and a navy T-shirt. Heading downstairs, I stuck a headband in my hair to hold it down. I went to bed with it wet last night. It wasn't my best look, but considering I barely slept and Charlie didn't know I existed, I wasn't going to worry about it.

Mom met me at the bottom of the stairs with a cinnamon roll.

"Greta Grace, I really wish you would sit down to a proper breakfast in the morning. Breakfast fuels your brain until lunch, and quite honestly, I don't think this is the way to do that."

"I know, but I love these." I held the cinnamon roll between my teeth while I put on my shoes and swung my backpack over my shoulder. Mom handed me my lunch, kissed me goodbye, and shooed me out. She closed the door—then opened it again.

"Remember to count your blessings today!" she called after me.

"I will!" I yelled back, though today there was no way I was doing that. There didn't seem to be any blessings in my life lately! Plus, the last thing I wanted to hear right now was that "something good comes out of everything." Regardless of what Mom or Mrs. McGee would say, I could not see anything good coming out of Casey being on my back or Mrs. McGee getting a call from the cancer doctor!

"Okay, Greta Grace," Samantha said as she tucked her long blonde curls behind her ears and straightened her glasses. She wrapped her arm in mine, and we headed for the bus. "There's only one way out of this. Start getting some B's, maybe even a C here and there."

Pulling my arm back from her, I shook my head. "I can't do that."

"You have to. Who knows what she will have posted by tonight? Just consider it."

Samantha and I sat in the same two seats we always sat in. It was the fifth row from the front; me at the window, Samantha on the aisle. After scooting into my seat, I yawned and gazed out the dirty window of the bus. I couldn't imagine that life was meant to be this stressful. Sooner than I wanted, Samantha elbowed me that it was time to get off. I dreaded today. I wish I had faked being sick.

Samantha gathered up her things. "Maybe she'll get hit by a car," she said, "and we won't have to worry about her."

"Whoa, Samantha. Good thing you don't really mean that because that would be bad news for you." I finished tying my shoes and gave her a look.

"Is it bad to wish that she would gently die in her sleep?"

I couldn't believe she said that. "Yeah," I told her. "Still bad."

Samantha looked utterly confused. "With everything she has done and is still doing, is it really that bad to want to be rid of her?"

The bus crawled to a stop. "Think of the Golden Rule," I said. "You know, the one that says, 'do unto others as you would have done unto you.' Kind of like, you get what you give."

"Whatever." Samantha shrugged.

We got off the bus, and Samantha took off like a bullet. Gripping my backpack to keep up with her, I asked. "Who did your aunt go to when she had cancer?"

Samantha stopped to pick up the school newspaper. "Dr. Klyne. Everyone knows he's the cancer guy." She started counting on her fingers. "My aunt went to him, and so did my mom's friend, and your grandmother too." She stopped and looked at me. "Why do you want to know?"

"It's Mrs. McGee. Yesterday, I was at her house and Dr. Klyne left a message." I could barely keep up with

Samantha. "Slow down! How do those short legs move so fast?"

"First of all, you're pretty much the same height, and we are just petite, not short, and secondly..." She imitated our homeroom teacher's squeaky, high-pitched voice. "Samantha Lynch, if you are late to my homeroom one more time, I am afraid you will have to stay for detention."

Back to her normal voice, Samantha complained, "Why is it that we both walk in at the exact same time, but she only wants to give me a detention? I'm pretty sure it's because she couldn't stand my two older brothers when she had them. Anyway, Mrs. McGee is fine. What did your mom say about it?"

"She had a ton of work stuff to do so I didn't ask her, but this is driving me crazy. How do I stop thinking about it?" I looked over at her and waited for her answer.

"Sorry, girl. I don't know. Anyway, don't you have some kind of meditation or yoga pose you do for that? She'll be fine. Right now, just concentrate on Casey Cunningham."

The bell rang. Just in time!

Chapter 5

WHAT A WAY TO START THE DAY. First period with Casey Cunningham. Though I pretended I couldn't see her, it was virtually impossible to miss that tall body of hers and that one lonely red ringlet hanging down on her forehead as the rest of her hair exploded from a high ponytail on top of her head. As soon as I sat down, a note was passed up until it got to me. It read:

> YOU WILL LET ME COPY FOR THE
> SPELLING TEST... OR ELSE!

Shoot! What was I going to do?

"Mrs. Kenneth, may I please go to the bathroom?"

I gave Samantha the nod, and she got permission to leave the room too. She darted into the hallway, and I showed her the note.

"Let her copy until we can figure out what to do." Samantha crumpled up the note.

"What if I get caught?" I threw my arms up in the air. "I just can't do that!"

Grabbing hold of my shoulders, she whispered, "You won't get caught. Mrs. Kenneth would never suspect you of cheating."

I looked down the long corridor and wished I could run out the door at the end of it and never come back. Mrs. Kenneth poked her smiling face out the door. "Girls, we are ready. Please come join us."

I went back in and sat down. I wanted to throw up.

"Number one," said Mrs. Kenneth. "Please spell the word 'manipulate.'"

I slanted my paper just enough for Casey to see, but not enough for Mrs. Kenneth to have reason to put a big "F" on the top of mine for cheating. After a couple of words, my hands were smudging the ink with sweat and my heart was pounding. I couldn't take it anymore. I covered my paper. Casey cleared her throat. I looked at her out of the corner of my eye. She gave me a mean look. I panicked, looked at her again, looked at my paper, looked at Mrs. Kenneth, and turned my paper to let her cheat again. Then, I didn't know if it was my imagination, but it felt like Mrs. Kenneths' eyes were on me. I turned the test back toward me and covered it up for the last four words. At the end of the test, Casey whispered, "You'll be sorry."

"Detention for talking, Casey," said Mrs. Kenneth. "I will see you after school."

Chapter **6**

Once again, Charlie did not notice me on the bus, and once again Samantha and I parted ways at the corner of Acorn and Wellington. I stood leaning up against the street sign and watched the bus drive off while Samantha headed down the road behind it. It was just starting to drizzle, but I didn't mind it at all. I looked up to the clouds and just let it run down my face.

Three months. How am I going to get through three more months of school? Maybe I should tell Mrs. McGee.

"Mrs. McGee, are you home?" I knocked on her front door. No response. I went around and knocked on the back door. When I got no answer, I grabbed her garbage can and carried it to the living room window, climbing up on it so I could look inside the house. Even though the rain was trickling down her window, I could see she was asleep on her brown leather recliner with Rudy on her lap. *That's strange. She never sleeps at this time of day.*

I hopped down, put her garbage can away, and grabbed her newspaper off of her lawn and stuck it in her door, then headed home. I had that gut feeling that something was wrong. I hated that feeling.

As I reached our little yellow house, I could see the light on. Unlike every other day, the paper had been picked up from the driveway and someone had taken the recycling bin in.

"Mom, why are you home from work so early?"

"Sweetheart, I took Mrs. McGee to the doctor today."

I gave her that strange "what are you talking about" kind of look.

"I'm sure it's nothing serious, but she has a lump that the doctor is going to check out. He's just being cautious."

"But it could be something, right? I mean, cancer can start out as a lump, right? I totally remember them saying it could be nothing with Grandma and she died." I headed through the living room, throwing, well, more like slamming, my backpack on the living room chair. "They tell everyone that."

Mom followed me into the kitchen. "It may be nothing. Lots of people have lumps that are not cancerous. They are going to do a biopsy and then they will be able to confirm that for us."

"I don't believe you. You didn't even tell me you were bringing her to the doctor, so why should I believe it's nothing?"

"I didn't want to tell you because I knew you would worry, and there was nothing you could do about it at school. I promise, Greta Grace, I don't know any more right now than you do."

Opening the cabinet door, I pulled out a glass. "I bet she's scared out of her mind, and I should have helped." I poured myself half a glass of milk and sat at the kitchen table. I buried my face in my hands.

"Greta Grace, it's okay." Mom bent down as she wrapped her arms around my shoulders.

I tried to speak through the tears. "I was there when the doctor left the message, and I should have told her, but I didn't know how, and so I didn't, but I should have." I pulled my feet up on the chair and my knees into my chest. "God, first Casey, now Mrs. McGee. I can't stand this." I drank some milk.

It had started to rain harder.

"Honey, slow down. Casey who? And what is going on with her?"

"Let's just say Casey Cunningham doesn't like people who get A's."

"That's ridiculous. I am sure the guidance counselor or principal can help us sort this out."

Why did I open my big mouth?

"You cannot go to the principal. Promise me you won't go to the principal." I looked at her with forbidding eyes.

"But why, Greta Grace? There is no way I am going to let someone get away with bullying you, and there is no way you are going to spend your days dodging a bully."

"No! Don't do that. You will make things a million times worse. I can handle it." I got up and put my glass in the dishwasher. The rain was getting worse.

"If it isn't better by the end of tomorrow, then I will be making a call myself." She stood, waiting for my answer. She had that look on her face that told me she was dead serious.

"Fine. Give it to the end of tomorrow." *Maybe Samantha was right. Maybe I needed to start getting some B's and C's.*

And then Mom went on with what she called her words of wisdom. "Greta Grace, you are amazing, strong, loveable and beautiful with an inner bright light shining that cannot be dimmed. That's who you are. Not even Casey Cunningham can change that!"

"Yeah, I know."

Mom gave me one of those extra-long hugs.

"I've got to go see Mrs. McGee. I'll be back by dinner." I dried my eyes off on my sleeve and grabbed my raincoat.

Chapter 7

OKAY, THINK ABOUT WHAT YOU ARE GOING TO SAY. I stood outside Mrs. McGee's house, blinking rain out of my eyes. *What's the right thing to say?* "Hi, Mrs. McGee. How are you?" *She might be sick. What did I expect her to say?* I thought again. "Hello, Mrs. McGee. I am so sorry I didn't warn you about the message that day from your doctor." Or "Hi, Mrs. McGee. Please, please don't die."

The light yellow door to her house opened, followed by the screen door.

"My sweet girl, are you going to come in out of that dreadful rain, or do you think you'll grow a few more inches by standing in it?" She folded her arms to ward off the rain that was blowing her way as I climbed the stairs to her house. She was in a good mood, so maybe it was all just a big mistake.

I took off my soaked shoes, left them on the mat, hung up my coat on the extra hook that became mine a long time ago, and followed her into the kitchen.

"How about a cup of hot chocolate? I was going to cook your favorite muffins for after school today, but silly me fell asleep." She washed her hands, dried them off on her apron, pulled out two big mugs, and put the kettle on.

"Mrs. McGee." I pulled out the chair at the kitchen table and sat down. "I heard the message from the doctor when I was getting our drinks the other day, and I wanted to say something but didn't know how, so I didn't and, well, I should have." I looked up slowly and turned toward her to see if she heard or understood all the mumbo jumbo I had just said.

She put everything down and pulled out the chair next to me. "Oh goodness, Greta Grace. I hope you haven't been worrying about this. You didn't need to tell me about the message. I can handle any message that comes my way." She kissed both of my cheeks and went to turn off the boiling kettle.

I followed her and poured the hot chocolate mix into the cups. "Are you okay?"

"I am going to go in for a test, but I know I am going to be just fine. Molly McGee never gives up without a fight. Don't you remember? We have that in common."

Hmm. I didn't seem to be that person these days. In fact, I was anything but.

"I will do what I always do. I will turn this over to God. I am not going to worry and neither are you."

I just looked at her, begging for a promise—a total guarantee that she would be fine.

She grabbed my hands and started waltzing around the kitchen singing out loud, "I am going to be fine; so, so fine." She ended the dance with a big bear hug, and we laughed. I believed she was going to be fine; so, so fine.

Chapter 8

MOM FLUNG OPEN THE DOOR TO MY BEDROOM. "My goodness, Greta Grace. Are you ever ready for Samantha when she gets here?" I was ready. I charged down the stairs and out the front door.

"Hey, are you okay?" Samantha followed me out through the front gate of our house. "You look like something is wrong."

"Did you look at the postings this morning?" I handed her my phone.

She went pale when she read, "Go die, Greta Grace, and take Samantha with you!" The next one said, "Greta Grace Gibson, you may be smart, but you're a stupid LOSER!"

"Oh, my gosh! This is it. It's all downhill from here." Samantha handed me back my phone. "You *have* to do it. You have to start getting some B's and C's. Don't you see you don't have a choice?"

"I tried talking myself into doing that. I did. But I can't do it."

"Are you kidding me? Grades don't even matter at our age. You can get straight A's when they really count." She looked at me like I was an idiot.

"I swear, Samantha, I want to, but I just can't. I need a scholarship for college. I need to get into some advanced classes for high school—and what if they think I'm not capable?"

Samantha shook her head. "Do you realize she can and will make our, I mean your, life miserable? She will chew you up and spit you out like an old piece of gum." She rolled her eyes and started kicking a stone down the street.

I watched the stone disappear into the grass. "Maybe I should just show someone what she posted and let them take care of it."

"Believe me, she's never gotten caught, so you'll make things worse. You've gotta consider getting some bad grades."

"And if she doesn't like the way I dress, should I change that too? And then, if she doesn't like the color of my hair, should I change that? Don't you get it? It'll never end." I shrugged my shoulders like it was no big deal, even though secretly it scared me to death. "Anyway," I went on, "you know how I always say that angels give us signs through numbers? Well, for the last three nights I've woken up a lot thinking about this, but every time I woke up, I saw three digits—first 1:11, then 4:44 and then 5:55. I know it was a sign from the angels that this is the right thing to do."

"You and your stupid three digits and your stupid visualizations and angel talk. You're getting weirder by the day!" Samantha wouldn't look at me.

"Really? You didn't think visualizing was so lame when you played your best season ever at softball this year. Wasn't so lame then, was it?"

"Fine. Do what you want!" She stormed off ahead of me.

"Fine, and don't think I don't know that you're not worried about what she'll do to me. You're worried that she'll do something to you!"

"Forget it. Do what you want!" She crossed over to the other side of the street to make it clear, like it wasn't already, that we were officially having a fight.

I made it to the bus in record time. So did Samantha, who was sitting in our seats with her on again, off again friend Lucy. Obviously, today she was on.

I scanned the bus for an open seat. *God! Could this day get any worse?*

"Take a seat, dear." Joe, the bus driver, waited for me as he rolled up a sleeve, took a bite of his bagel, leaving a cream cheese mustache, and hit the lever to shut the door.

No way! Don't even tell me the only seat left is next to Charlie. My gaze darted up and down the rows, looking for anywhere else to sit. I walked toward the only empty seat.

Charlie looked up from his iPhone. "Hey."

"Hi. Uh… Looks like my regular seat is gone." I half-smiled, half-apologized.

"Sure." He moved his backpack off the seat and stuffed it under the one in front of him so I could sit.

Stay calm. Stay cool. I kicked my backpack under the seat in front of me.

He was zapping away at the buttons, making figures run all over the screen.

"Do you know how to play this?" He glanced at me in between zaps.

"Nope." I didn't even know the name of the game. Mom's theory about games being a waste of time was just blown out of the water.

"Here, it's easy. Just push this and try to get this guy to the end without letting any of the figures jump on him. If you get stuck, fire back using this button." He handed the game over to me.

My heart was skipping beats. I don't know what made me more nervous, trying this game that I knew nothing about or having him sit so close to me. *God, I wish I didn't like him so much.*

"Keep going. You're almost at the next level."

I poked around at it for a while, and I did it! "I knocked them all out," I told Charlie. Handing the game back to him, I got a glimpse of his really blue eyes and for just one second I forgot that life wasn't okay.

"Just in time." He smiled, stood up, grabbed his backpack, his baseball bat and glove, and followed me off of the bus. Flinging his blonde bangs to one side, he said, "See you later."

Charlie was the cutest boy I had ever seen. I had to tell Samantha about this. Oh, right. I forgot. We weren't talking.

Chapter 9

CASEY WAS CRAMMING HER BOOKS INTO HER LOCKER. That wouldn't have been so bad, except she was standing three lockers away from me. My heart was racing. She stopped and stared me down. I pretended I couldn't care less, though my wobbly knees might have given me away. I couldn't stand it, so I decided to forget dealing with my locker and carry all my books around for the day.

Samantha and Lucy were walking down the hallway. No way was I going to let Samantha think Lucy bothered me. She didn't see me ganging up on her every time I got mad, did she? I had plenty of other friends to hang out with.

Or maybe I didn't. As I walked by Samantha to get to my classroom, she had our entire group huddled around her. No doubt, I was the topic of conversation.

Clearly, she needed to make sure everyone was on her side before they ever heard mine. Ugh!

Throughout the day, I acted braver than I felt and ignored Casey and her looks and comments, even when I was crying inside.

Once again, I hopped on the bus and Lucy was sitting right there in my seat. *Really? Doesn't she get it? The only time she's in that seat is when Samantha is mad at me. But fine. Go ahead and sit in it.*

"Hey, empty seat here." Charlie pointed to the seat next to him. I looked behind me to see if he was talking to someone else. *Oh, my gosh! He's talking to me.*

Samantha and Lucy turned to look. *Hmm. Something good may come out of this fight after all.* "Oh, thanks. Where's Mikey today?" This had been his seat for the last three years.

"He has the flu or something. Why were you kicked out of your seat?"

"Girl drama." I looked over at my former best friend in the seat across the aisle.

"Girls are always so dramatic."

Not knowing what to say without sounding dramatic, I just shrugged.

He poked at his phone for a minute, then looked at me like I had just gotten there. "Hey, do you want to go fishing tomorrow?"

Wow! Of course I'd go fishing. I'd go wading in lava with Charlie. "Um, sure," I managed to say. "I've never fished before, though." *Not looking good. Never played the video game, never fished.*

"That doesn't matter. I'll bring an extra rod. I'll be at the lake at one o'clock."

I could hardly breathe. "So," I said, like it was no big thing. "I'll see you tomorrow afternoon at one."

I got off the bus with Samantha behind me. No pinky swear followed by a shoulder nudge and high five. Just silence from Samantha—and a date with Charlie that I couldn't even tell her about.

But I could tell Mrs. McGee. I picked up a handful of daisies that were clumped up in little bouquets on the ground and tossed them in the air. I took off to her house. She would be so excited to hear my news! I never thought this day would come!

Chapter 10

THERE WAS A LOT GOING ON around Mrs. McGee's house. I went and hid behind the huge cherry blossom tree across the street, making sure I could see but that no one could see me. There was that feeling in my stomach again. I just knew something was wrong.

The Massachusetts license plates on the cars in the driveway meant her son and daughter were there. Doors were slamming; kids ran in and out of her house. A tall scrawny girl in pink high-tops and bright orange shorts chased Rudy through the garden, trampling flowers. She tossed Mrs. McGee's pink gardening hat in the air and then caught it repeatedly.

"Get out of her flowers. Stop chasing Rudy," I muttered. As the tall scrawny girl tossed Mrs. McGee's hat into the air one more time, I yelled, "Put her hat back!"

The scrawny girl stopped in her tracks and looked across the street. "Who is that?" She crept closer to the sidewalk like an animal that didn't want to scare away its prey.

I didn't move.

"I heard you. Who are you?" She put her hands on her hips and stood looking in my direction.

I stepped out. "I'm Greta Grace."

"So, you're Greta Grace. You're the girl my grandmother always talks about. Who do you think you are, telling me what to do?"

"Do you even know how much time she spent on that garden?"

"Whatever." The girl rolled her eyes, tossed her hair, and walked away as she placed the hat on her head.

"Nice, real nice!" I yelled and then took off like a cheetah. I had to get home to see if Mom was there.

· · · · ·

"Good, you're home, Greta Grace. I just came back from the hospital to get you, so you could see Mrs. McGee. Her family will be there later, so this would be a good time for you to go." She was rushing around, straightening up the kitchen, even though there was nothing out of place. She then pulled a hairbrush out of her purse to comb her hair. I could tell something was wrong; so, so wrong.

I felt the color drain from my face. "Why? What happened?" I put down the package of cookies I had just opened. "Why is she in the hospital?"

"Well, when I went to pick up Mrs. McGee this morning to take her for that test I told you about, she was lying unconscious at the bottom of the stairs. She must have slipped and fallen down them and hit her head because she had a cut on it. But we don't really know why she fell because she's in a coma."

I had never heard of that before, but Mom said it's kind of like when someone falls asleep and can't wake up. It's weird because you don't know when they're going to wake or if they even will.

The thought of that happening to Mrs. McGee made me cry. "Will she be alright?"

Mom wrapped her arms around me. "Yes, I am sure she will. It'll be okay, sweetie. You know, maybe I should just go today, and you can go when you're feeling a bit better about it, or when Mrs. McGee wakes up. Clearly, I didn't think this through very well."

"No, she needs me. She might wake up if she hears me. I'm going." I put away the cookies I was going to eat. I didn't want them anymore.

Mom picked up her gigantic brown purse—the purse that on a good day I would make fun of her for—grabbed her keys and headed toward the back door. "Are you sure?"

"Yeah, I'm sure." I followed her to the car, and we were out of the driveway in a flash.

I looked over at her. "I sure hope that hospital knows what it's doing. I remember what it did to Grandma. One day she was sick, the next day she was in there, and a month later she was dead. I think that hospital kills people."

I bit my nails, not that there was much left to bite after worrying about Casey, and looked out the window of the car. The daisies no longer looked like beautiful bouquets, and the sun didn't really seem like it was shining that brightly anymore. My new view on life had lasted for about five minutes. "Hospitals spook me."

Chapter 11

THE TWO STEEL DOORS LEADING INTO THE HOSPITAL looked like something that belonged to a prison. Well, at least like the ones I see on TV. *What if they never let her out of here? Nothing about this place feels safe.*

"The ammonia smell, the white walls, the bulky beds. It all really makes me want to pass out." I looked at Mom to make sure she knew how serious I was.

"I know this is hard for you." She grabbed my cheeks in her hands, looked straight into my eyes, and planted a kiss on my forehead. Then, she took me by the hand like I was a two-year-old.

"We're looking for Molly McGee," Mom said to the short, white-haired, grumpy-looking lady sitting at the front desk. She turned to her computer, typed in the name, and without even looking up, abruptly answered,

"Room 202. Down the hall, up the elevator, and two doors down on the right."

"See, Mom? Even she doesn't like this place, and she works here."

"Well then, there's an excellent lesson learned today. You probably don't want to work in a hospital when you get older. Here we go, Room 202."

Mom pushed the door open. I felt like someone had drop-kicked my heart and then stepped on it and squashed it. Mrs. McGee lay motionless on the bed. She looked awful. Her rosy cheeks and pink lips actually looked gray. A thin, ugly, light blue hospital gown replaced her usual flowery skirts and matching blouses.

She looked like she was at least one hundred years old.

"Hi, Mrs. McGee." I spoke softly and walked over to her bed. It took everything in me not to cry.

I wondered if you could be scared while you were in a coma. I pulled up a chair beside her bed. My heart ached as I took her hand.

"I hope you're okay. That must have been so scary to fall like that." I wiped the tears from my eyes. "I'll save all the crossword puzzles out of the paper for you," I whispered.

Mrs. McGee would always say, "Greta Grace, even at my age, it's important to keep your mind stimulated. Never forget that." I had to help her do that now. What if they didn't stimulate her mind while she was here, and she didn't remember anything? What if she didn't even remember me?

Her eyes stayed shut as I sat holding her hand, breathing deeply so I wouldn't cry. I watched her eyes, waiting to see if they would open, but they didn't.

After a while, Mom came in. "Greta Grace, it's time to let Mrs. McGee's daughter come in now." Mom walked over to Mrs. McGee and took her hand.

I got up, stepped back, and peeked around the curtain that divided the room to see the woman who was in the other bed. I wondered if she was already dead and nobody knew it yet. She was straight as a board with her eyes shut tight, and she didn't even look like she was breathing. Is it possible that they wouldn't know if she died? *I know what this hospital does to people. She probably is dead. Mrs. McGee has to get out of here.*

A nurse with crystal blue eyes and blonde curls pulled back in a ponytail, whose name tag said Megan, walked in with more of Mrs. McGee's family. *At least that scrawny girl isn't here.*

I walked over and kissed Mrs. McGee on the cheek. "I love you." I blinked away my tears.

"She'll be okay." Mom put her arm around my shoulders and squeezed me close as we walked down a long hospital hall of white walls.

"I'm not little anymore, so you can tell me if you think she might not be okay. You said you would be honest with me. I can handle it."

"I know this is hard, Greta Grace. Even I'm having a hard time with it. We'll just have to trust she'll be okay." She looked at me, wrinkled her brow, and pulled me even closer to her.

Maybe I wasn't so mature. Every ounce of me felt afraid.

Chapter 12

"MOM, I'LL BE BACK BY 3 P.M. TO GO SEE MRS. MCGEE." I shouted up the stairs, waiting for her to come to the landing to answer.

"Where are you going?" She had that smirk on her face that meant she already knew.

"Fishing. Remember, I told you on the way home last night."

Still smiling, she said, "Right, with that boy, Charlie. Do you think those sneakers are appropriate for fishing?"

"Yeah, they're fine." I looked at the time on my phone. I needed to get out of here. *Please don't ask any more questions.*

"I'm sure he's a very nice boy, but remember, Greta Grace, you always want to be with someone who treats you with respect and who is proud to be with you."

"Um. Okay. Not sure where this is all coming from, but that's fine."

"Well, I just hear so many stories these days about dating at your age, and I want to make sure that you realize how worthy you are."

"Oh my gosh, Mom." I rolled my eyes. "I'm not marrying him. I'm going fishing with him. Big difference."

"Okay. Enough of that. On another note, did Samantha mention anything about their house being on the market?"

"No. She hasn't said anything." *It would be hard to know something about someone who doesn't talk to you.* I opened the screen door to let her know in the nicest way possible that I needed to leave.

She followed me out to the porch, gave me a big squeeze hug, and then sat down on the steps to watch me ride off on my bike.

Over the hill, left on the next road, another half mile down the road, and before I knew it, I could see him sitting on one of the boulders that overlooked the lake.

Oh, why weren't Samantha and I talking? Who hangs out with their biggest crush without telling their best friend? I hopped off of my bike and slid it into the empty slot in the bike rack.

"You can do this," I coached myself. I tossed my hair to make it a little fluffier, put my headband back on, tucked my shirt in and then untucked it, and walked over to where I saw Charlie sitting.

"Hey, what's up?" I sat down next to him on the boulder. There were stone walls surrounding a wide open shimmering body of water. Towels were spread out on whatever flat boulders could be found, with people all around tanning, fishing or having a picnic. It felt like a vacation, which I actually hadn't been on in a really long time.

"Hey." He looked up and smiled. He'd hooked a fat worm at the end of a fishing line.

"Sure is pretty here." I smiled, leaned back on my hands and tilted my head up to the sun. That was until I heard Mrs. McGee's voice in the back of my mind saying, "Your skin will thank you for staying out of the sun."

"Yeah, it's a pretty popular place." Charlie checked and then re-checked the rod to make sure it was all set and then handed it to me. "My dad, my sister, and I come here all the time. They're right over there." He pointed directly across from us to a little girl with blonde pigtails and a man who was a grown-up version of Charlie.

"Hmm. Must be nice to do stuff like this with a dad." I said it out loud without really meaning to. That man was not someone I *ever* talked about.

"Are your parents divorced?" He looked up from the rod.

"Yeah." Enough said.

He came and stood right next to me. He was the perfect height, not too tall and not too short. I couldn't imagine me dating someone who was a lot shorter than me. Mom would have a lot to say about how shallow that is. The sun beamed on the water, and here I was with Charlie. What could be more perfect than this? Except of course having a best friend again.

Chapter 13

"THANKS FOR THE SEAT ON THE BUS." That seemed like a good way to start the conversation.

"You and what's-her-name in a fight?" He sat and held the rod in between his knees and started digging his hand through his pocket. He pulled out two pieces of gum and handed one to me.

I propped myself up next to him. "Her name is Samantha. Do you actually even know my name?"

"Of course I do. It's Margaret, right? No, no, I mean, Megan? Yeah, I know your name, but it's too long. I'm just going to call you GG."

I laughed. This was turning out to be way easier than I expected.

"Anyway, Casey has picked me as her next target. She doesn't like A students. Samantha wants me to mess up a few grades. I think she thinks that if Casey goes after me, she'll go after her too."

"You're probably right because Samantha actually chose to be Casey's partner in science."

"Really? She chose to be her partner? That's messed up."

Just then, he jumped up. "You've got one!" He pointed at the pole. "Reel it in."

I was thrilled. Not only was it easy to hang out with Charlie, but obviously, I was a natural at this fishing thing.

Until my foot slipped.

With nothing to grab, I was in the air, legs and arms flailing about, headband flying off, while the fishing pole shot through the air like a torpedo, just before I landed in the lake.

"These stupid, slippery shoes." I looked up at him from the water.

He ran and grabbed my pole out of the water.

"Are you okay? I've never seen anyone fall in before." He bent over the rocks to pull my headband from the water.

I grabbed onto a rock, pulled my humiliated self up, and squeezed the water out of my drenched white T-shirt. "Nobody would be a big enough klutz to do that but me."

"No, no. I mean, it's not a big deal."

Everybody knows that a wet white T-shirt is never a good thing. "I've got to get out of here." I ran to my bike.

"Take my sweatshirt." Charlie grabbed it off of the ground and handed it to me.

I immediately stopped. "Is that Casey over there?" I squinted and nodded to the other side of the lake.

She was hysterical, bent over laughing, holding her stomach and pointing directly at me.

"Oh, my gosh. I have to go." I ran to my bike, got on it, and pedaled away. I didn't stop until I got home.

Chapter **14**

"GRETA GRACE, WHAT HAPPENED, LOVEY?" When Mom used the word "lovey," I knew I looked as bad as I felt.

"What happened is that I fell in and Casey was there, and I don't want to talk about it." On the verge of tears, I went straight up the stairs and grabbed the phone. I needed Samantha. Fight or no fight, we would always be there for each other. Her phone rang. It went to voicemail.

"Hi, Samantha. It's me. Please call me. I really don't know what to do about Casey and guess what? I went fishing with Charlie, and I fell in the lake. Not only did I fall in, but Casey was there—and Mrs. McGee is in the hospital. So, yeah." My voice quivered. I barely got the rest of the sentence out. "Please call me."

I was ready to collapse into a puddle of tears, but I stopped, closed my eyes, and took a deep breath. I just knew I would get a call within the next hour and we would meet at the stone wall halfway between her house and mine and we would talk, just like we always did. I breathed a sigh of relief, glad I made the call.

"Greta Grace." Mom came in and sat at the foot of my bed while I rifled through my drawers to find something dry to put on. "I absolutely will not sit and do nothing if Casey is still intimidating you. You told me she had backed off, and that it was over."

I couldn't look at her because she would know I was lying. I looked in the mirror, grabbed a brush, and started brushing my hair. "She did."

I could tell by the way she stayed quiet that she wasn't sure if she should believe me. "Trust me."

I loved Mom, but her strategy scared me. She would go to the school. They were all about "conflict resolution." Yeah, that would work. Let's put me and Casey in the same room to talk about our problem. Then she could just make it a point to get me after school, which would be even worse.

"Bullying is not acceptable... Ever. Got it?" She waited for me to nod my head yes and then moved on.

Phew.

"Where is Samantha these days? She hasn't been around at all."

"She goes to school early for extra help now, that's all." *Gosh, I would really have to redeem myself in church after all these lies.*

"One more thing. Mrs. McGee's daughter called to say that she is really weak today, so the doctors have limited her visitors to family."

I stood up straight. "We are her family. In fact, I am so way more family than that girl who was running through her flowers and throwing her hat around the place."

"I know, but they have driven a long way to spend time with her, and we need to respect that." She got up and started collecting the clothes from the floor by my bed. She picked up Charlie's sweatshirt, clearly recognized that it wasn't mine, folded it neatly and placed it on my desk chair. I went over to help her. I always felt guilty when she started cleaning up my stuff. "I don't like that scrawny girl."

She walked over and hugged me. "Come down when you're ready to eat. I really am sorry you had such a terrible afternoon." She paused for a minute, remembering. "Reminds me of the time I went on a roller coaster with a boy I liked. The second I got off, I vomited. Now that was embarrassing! I never was a roller coaster person."

I couldn't help but wonder if the boy she talked about was *that* guy; the one she had me with. As she hugged me, I breathed in the smell of her perfume. Strange, but it smelled soothing, and somehow it always made me feel safe. She's been wearing the same perfume for as long as I can remember, and I hope she never changes it.

"I promise there are good things to come, Greta Grace. Just have faith." She let go of me, tossed a sock that was hiding under my desk chair into the laundry basket, and proceeded out the door.

I grabbed the sweatshirt off my chair, sniffed it to see if it still smelled like Charlie, put it on, and threw myself onto my bed. I lay there and thought about how I dreaded the idea of going back to the hospital, with the same grumpy lady at the desk, Mrs. McGee stuck in that bed, and most likely, the bed next to her would be empty because that woman would certainly be dead by tomorrow. But for Mrs. McGee, I would go again and again and again.

Chapter 15

WHAT THE HECK? *Why didn't Samantha call? She would never let her phone run out of a charge. She had to have gotten my message.* I checked my phone again just to make sure I hadn't missed her call and then left for the bus stop.

"Well, that explains it." I stopped to watch. Standing on the corner, Casey, who normally never took the morning bus, was with her posse. They were hovering over the latest teen fashion magazine, with Samantha giggling beside them. I felt like someone punched me in the gut. Wow! This is what it had come to. She was actually choosing Casey over me. My heart sank right down to my toes. I couldn't have felt sadder.

Unfortunately for Charlie's friend Mikey, I needed him to still be out of school so I could have his seat. The only problem was that Charlie probably figured out yesterday that I'm not girlfriend material, maybe not even friend material.

Oh, my gosh. Mikey is back on the bus. The only empty seat was the "loser seat" at the front of the bus. It was a single seat that was directly behind the bus driver. Nobody ever sat there because there was nobody that was that big of a loser. Except me. That's what I felt like. I sat down, but not before I gave Samantha a very long, I-hate-you, dirty look.

"Hey, GG." Charlie stuck his head into the aisle and called up to me. "We can fit three to a seat."

"It's okay. Don't want you to get into trouble." *Shoot. Why did I say that? I've been lying like crazy to my mom and now I decide I have to follow all the rules?*

"Then catch!" He threw me a corn muffin. "I brought one from home for you. I remembered you said you liked them."

Actually, I said I don't like corn muffins, but I think I just fell in love.

"You guys! Everyone, listen! I have the funniest story to tell." Casey dramatically jumped up from the last seat on the bus.

"Oh, my gosh." I mouthed while looking over to Charlie. It didn't take a brain surgeon to know what was about to happen. If there was any way to bolt off a moving bus, I would have done it.

"She's going to make a fool out of me in front of the whole bus. Please, God, help me." I whispered to God, to Grandma, to the angels, to anyone up there who was listening.

Everyone eagerly awaited her big news because Casey, being Casey, demanded everyone's attention and everyone was too afraid not to give it. Samantha and Lucy were already laughing when I caught Samantha's eye and glared at her. She turned away so she could ignore the fact that I knew what she was doing. She got my message last night but decided to join "Team Casey." I hate her. I hate her! *I hate her!*

Joe, the bus driver, nipped it in the bud. "Casey Cunningham, put your butt in that seat and do not say one more word, or I'll officially kick you off my bus." His face got red as he glared at her in the rearview mirror.

She sat down, jeering at me, and laughing at the same time. I quickly looked away.

The fifteen-minute ride felt like fifteen hours. I never thought I'd be this happy to see bus doors open.

"C'mon, we'll walk you to class." Charlie and Mikey stood on either side of me like they were bodyguards.

"Hold on. I want to talk to Joe." I waited for everyone to get off of the bus, including Casey, who laughed at me as she walked by. I stepped back on to the bus, but before I could speak a word, Joe spoke. "Sure was a nice day at the lake on Saturday, huh?"

I buried my face in my hand. "Oh, no. Please tell me you weren't there too."

"Just there enjoying my fishing, not paying attention to anything else."

"Thanks, Joe."

He smiled, and I scurried off the bus. Hopefully, Joe had bought me some time; just maybe. Casey was smart enough to stay under the radar since Joe had figured her out.

Chapter 16

Mom's car was in the driveway when I got home from school, which meant there was either really good news about Mrs. McGee or really bad news. *Ahh! Maybe Mrs. McGee had woken up!* I ran into the house.

"Mom, I'm home." I kicked off my shoes and walked through the living room to see if she was in the kitchen. Lately, I found it hard to eat, but today, it all caught up with me, and I was starving.

There was a beautiful arrangement of prettily wrapped flowers on the kitchen countertop that I figured had to be for Mrs. McGee. Since she was probably awake, she would love something pretty to look at. They would definitely cheer up that miserable, dreary room of hers.

Mom walked in.

"Is she awake? Is that why you're home?" I poured my milk and happily sat down at the table.

"Oh gosh, no, Greta Grace. I just took a half day at work today."

"Seriously? When is she going to wake up? Shouldn't she be awake by now? Ugh! This is so frustrating!"

"It could take weeks Greta Grace. The important thing is not to give up."

Sadness turned to anger. "I would rather be unconscious too than be in that stupid hospital bed! I bet that woman in the bed next to her is dead. That hospital kills people! Do you believe me now? They don't want people to leave. Ever! They probably have no idea how to take care of her."

Mom stayed silent and just let me explode, like she had done a thousand times before. She picked up the flowers, walked out the door, and waited patiently until I joined her.

I got in the car. Bam! I couldn't slam the door hard enough. We drove past Mrs. McGee's house, and I thought about the hot days when we would water her flowers and hose Rudy down. Samantha always thought I was just "doing the right thing" by visiting Mrs. McGee all the time, but I loved being around her.

She would always say, "Greta Grace, you are like a breath of fresh air."

Then I would always say, "Mrs. McGee, you are like the sun after a thunderstorm."

Then we would laugh at how wonderful we both were.

Once again, we arrived at the gross, awful hospital, walked through the gross, awful hallway, and finally got to her gross, awful room.

"Oh, my gosh," I whispered. "She looks like she is dying." *Was she?* I looked at Mom. *Was she telling me everything she knew? Maybe she figured I couldn't really handle "honest" after all.*

Mrs. McGee's daughter and son-in-law were there, and Mom took a walk with them down the hall. *Were they talking about a secret they were keeping from me? Did they know more than Mom told me?*

But it was just me and Mrs. McGee now. The room was silent, not a single sound except for the hum of the monitor next to her bed. It felt spooky and cold and dark. It was the feeling I always imagined I'd have if I got locked in school overnight; kind of like that dungeon feeling.

Chapter 17

"MRS. MCGEE, IT'S ME, GRETA GRACE," I whispered, pulling a chair beside her bed. The scratching of the chair on the floor sounded ten times louder than normal in the silence. I picked up her hand in mine and held it really tight, as if the squeeze alone might wake her up.

"I don't know if you can hear me, but I think you can." I stood up and leaned in really close to her ear. "You can't die, Mrs. McGee. You know that, don't you? You don't even know what happened with Charlie or how much I need you to help me with Casey. Besides, what about Rudy? I'm sure he's confused with those other people in your house."

I stopped whispering and waited for her to answer. She had nothing to say back. I crawled onto the bed, still holding her hand. Still whispering, I spoke to her again. "This might help." I pulled out one of the crosswords from my pocket that I had saved for her. "We'll do this together. You're much better at this than I am, so jump in any time you feel like."

Every so often, I would stop and pause, just in case she decided to say something, but was met with only silence. I stopped and looked at her. Her eyes were closed tightly, like a lid on a jar that I couldn't get open. I put the crossword puzzle down.

No nail polish. No red lipstick. No fancy hair style. No words or sounds. *What was I doing? She wasn't going to answer me back.* I tried to stop the tears, but soon enough, they were sliding down my face and landing on her hand.

"Please don't die." I talked loudly right into her ear. "Please. Please don't leave me. Please wake up."

I looked around the room. Maybe she wasn't waking up because this room was so ugly. It was just cement walls painted white and a gray curtain separating her bed from the other half of the room.

"Mrs. McGee, we brought you a gigantic bouquet. They are really pretty. You'll really like them, but you have to open your eyes to see them. Please, please open your eyes."

Rain tapped on the window and slithered down the windowpanes, making sure there wasn't any sunlight.

"I know you don't want to stay here, but you have to wake up to come home. I'll take care of you if you just come home." I had to convince her to open her eyes.

The door flew open, and a tall man with a clipboard and stethoscope entered. "Hello, dear. If you don't mind leaving me with Molly, I need to examine her." He looked down at his chart and back up at me again. He disappeared behind the curtain separating the two beds.

I wiped my eyes on the sleeve of my shirt and hung my head so my watery eyes wouldn't be so obvious. I kissed Mrs. McGee on the cheek and then climbed off her bed. I stopped to listen.

The doctor was speaking to a woman on the other side of the curtain. He said, "I'm very sorry for your loss. She seemed like a remarkable woman."

"She was. She was the glue that held our family together. We'll be lost without her." The woman sniffled. I quietly pushed the door open and stepped outside of the room.

Oh, my gosh. That woman did die.

A chill ran through my entire body. I found the restroom around the corner, locked myself in the stall, and cried.

Soon I heard Mom's voice outside the stall. "Sweetie, it's Mom. Let's go home, baby."

I opened the stall door and collapsed into her arms. I couldn't imagine what people did without moms. Couldn't imagine Mrs. McGee's daughter, or even that scrawny girl with the braids, having to live without Mrs. McGee. Couldn't imagine Mom living without Mrs. McGee. Couldn't imagine me living without Mom. Couldn't imagine me living without Mrs. McGee.

Chapter 18

"HEY, GG! SIT WITH US." Charlie stuck his head out into the aisle of the bus.

"Another day in that loser seat was more than I could bear. Move over and let me in." Thank goodness for Charlie, but the hope that Joe had gotten me off Casey's radar came to a screeching halt as soon as we got to school.

Just because there had been no postings or public humiliation for the last day didn't mean anything. We walked up the stairs, and there, in red lipstick across my locker, were the words:

TRY HARD, LOOOOOOOOOSER!

A circle of five girls, including Casey, were standing in the corner, laughing. Samantha was on the outskirts of the group, close enough to be in it, but far enough to play it safe.

"Here, use this." Charlie offered me a balled-up T-shirt.

"No, I'm not going to use your T-shirt." But Charlie ferociously cleaned off my locker with it.

Charlie, Mikey and I stood at my locker, and Samantha and a group of girls passed right by me. As I watched them walk down the hallway, I felt like I was standing under a huge waterfall, with streams of loneliness and sadness gushing over me. Tears started to fall.

"Don't worry. You've still got us as friends." Charlie nudged my shoulder and half-smiled. Mikey nodded his head in agreement.

I tried to smile, but I couldn't bring myself to speak. I walked by Samantha and the rest of the girls, who had stopped in the hall, faking whatever confidence I could muster up with admittedly a gaping hole in my heart and a bucketful of fear. I think I was starting to crack.

By lunch, everyone was buzzing about what Casey had done, but then the second surprise for the day came. My lunch table, my "group," had merged with Casey's lunch table, so they were now one big happy family. I sat down at a table by myself.

Charlie yelled out, "GG, sit here." As he said it, the entire table of girls glared at me. It was easy to see Casey's face go red as she pursed her lips and called the girls to lean in as if they were having a conference. *Maybe the rumors about Casey liking Charlie were really true.*

"No, I'm good. I have work I have to do anyway." *How could I sit with him? If Casey really did like him, I would be putting an even bigger target on my back.* I looked over at Samantha to see if she was even slightly aware of how this must feel. She just kept laughing her fake laugh with the rest of my fake friends. Charlie and Mikey came over with their lunch to sit with me.

"You can't sit here. I think Casey likes you and, if she does, she'll make things worse for me if she sees you here. Go eat lunch at your table." I sounded like a mad mother.

"We can handle her." Charlie sounded confident and pulled out a chair.

"No. Go back to your table." They hesitated, but they listened to me and left.

Chapter 19

I SPENT LUNCH BY MYSELF, pretending that I was working on an assignment when I was actually writing a letter to God. It was short and simple, and I just wrote it over and over again. I figured writing it multiple times might make it more powerful. Probably not, but it was worth a try.

> Dear God,
> I know you hear me. Please tell me
> what to do or send me help.
> Love, Greta Grace

Before I had my answer, though, I would just have to make it through school, go to lacrosse, which was starting today, and then head over to see Mrs. McGee.

Maybe she would wake up today and then she could help me.

At 3 p.m., the bell finally rang. I waited for Casey to go to her locker and leave before I went to mine and then hurried to the gym, even though I would be the last one on the field. I raced in and started to change, but I recognized the voices on the other side of the lockers. "Okay, you guys. Party on Saturday night at Sarah's house. No Greta Grace." I knew that was Casey's voice.

Next, I heard Samantha. "Are you kidding? I would never invite her. Do you see how she's all over Charlie? Casey, you are such a better choice for him. You guys don't even know how long she's liked him. He probably just feels sorry for her."

One tear, two tears, three and then four. Wiping my nose with the back of my hand, I took a deep breath and walked around to the other side of the lockers. I glared at Samantha and started to walk off, but then stopped. Right before I pushed open the door that led out to the fields, I turned back and asked clearly, "When did you get to be so mean, Samantha?" Then, I walked out.

It felt like one of those dividers you see in a limo to separate the driver from the passengers came down. Only this one was blocking my heart from Samantha. Never again. Never, ever again, would she get a piece of it. Nope. This is not at all the way Mrs. McGee or Mom would have handled things, but you know what? Right now, my heart hurt too much to even think about it.

"Hey, Greta Grace. What's wrong?" Charlie stopped to let the rest of the baseball team go by him.

"Can't talk. Gotta get to the game or my coach will bench me for the start of it." I could feel that quivering, just-about-to-cry thing again. That was way, way too common these days. I swallowed back tears. "Then I have to go to the hospital after the game—to visit somebody."

"Okay. We'll go to the second half after our practice." He turned to Mikey to make sure he was good with doing that.

Mikey shrugged. "Yeah, sure."

I have to say, I had an awesome game. Okay, so maybe it had a bit to do with Charlie sitting on the sidelines.

Charlie and Mikey met me outside the school's entrance. "Great game. Didn't think you were so good."

"Okay. I think that might be a compliment?" I looked at him. *Seriously, who wouldn't have a good game if they knew Charlie Tierney was on the sidelines watching them?*

"It was. Yeah, I mean, I just didn't know."

"That's because you didn't know I existed." I gave him a sarcastic smile and changed my cleats to flip-flops.

"Yeah, I did, I just didn't..."

"You should probably stop talking right about now," I warned him.

He smiled. He and Mikey circled around on their bikes as I walked beside them.

"So, who is it you're going to the hospital to see?" Mikey asked.

"Mrs. McGee. She's like my grandmother, just not by blood. She's in a coma."

Mikey stopped on his bike and pulled out a bag half full of watermelon-flavored hard candies from his backpack. "You guys want one?" He passed the bag to Charlie and then on to me. "Greta Grace," he said, "just so you know. My grandfather was in a coma. He woke up, and he's fine."

"Thanks, Mikey."

Getting to the hospital seemed a lot quicker with them than by myself. I looked up at the front of the huge, old cement building standing in front of us. "God, I hope she gets out of here soon."

Double-stepping the stairs up to the hospital door, I turned to wave and watch them ride off. Mom and Mrs. McGee always said something good comes out of everything. Who would have thought that Charlie and Mikey would be my something good out of something very, very bad?

Chapter 20

MRS. MCGEE'S DAUGHTER met me inside the hospital lobby every day, and then while I visited she went to the cafeteria to eat and do some stuff for her job.

"Okay, Mrs. McGee," I said, climbing up on her bed. "Today, we have science homework to do, but first let me text Mom to let her know I'm here." I sent a quick text to Mom and started to pull my books out of my backpack, but then changed my mind and dropped them on the floor.

"Actually, I am just going to lie here next to you and talk." I leaned back against the pillows and started. "There's a lot going on, Mrs. McGee. Besides Charlie and Mikey, I have no friends. They all abandoned me. I walked in on Samantha's conversation today." I tried to hold back the tears. "There's a party and guess who isn't invited? I'm always waiting for Casey to do something or say something, but mostly, I'm getting really scared because I know the longer you stay like this, the less chance you have of waking up. You are not going to leave me, right? I mean, you just wouldn't do that." I held her hand and rested my head on her shoulder. *What was I going to do if she never woke up?*

"Do you mind if I come in?" Megan, the same nurse who was always there, poked her head in.

"Sure. Come on in." I assumed she had to check on Mrs. McGee, but instead she pulled up a chair.

"I think she's a very lucky lady to have a girl like you in her life, and I would say you are probably just as lucky to have her, huh?"

"Yeah." I knew she meant well, but what she said made me want to cry.

"I bet this is challenging for you. If you ever need to talk, just come grab me. I work this shift every school day. Can I get you a soda, water or maybe a snack? There are some donuts out at the nurse's station, and I always have a stash of chocolate if you'd prefer that."

"I'm good, but thanks. I'm just going to sit with her and wait for her to wake up."

"Okay. You just call me if you think of anything I can do." She smiled.

"Thanks." I couldn't help but think that, if she has kids, I'd bet she's a really nice mom.

Like she did every day, Mom came to visit Mrs. McGee and pick me up. Sitting on the bed beside me, she held my hand and Mrs. McGee's, and we said a prayer.

For weeks, I followed the same routine. I went to school, listened to Casey's mean comments, ate lunch by myself, went to lacrosse, and then walked with Charlie and Mikey to the hospital. Every single day, I climbed on her bed with my homework, and every single day, Mom and I left without Mrs. McGee making a sound. I was getting scared that people would give up on her.

Finally, one day on our way to the hospital, Charlie did.

"Greta Grace, do you think Mrs. McGee will come out of this? It seems like a long time."

I stared at him. "Don't you ever say that again," I screamed. "That's just stupid. Never say that again." I took off running. Charlie and Mikey rode to catch up with me. I ran faster.

"Greta Grace, wait! I'm sorry. I didn't mean it like that."

I finally reached the hospital steps and sat down and cried. "What if she doesn't wake up? What if you're right? What if I'm the stupid one?" I sniffed and tried to catch the tears before they rolled down my cheeks. I looked up at him. "I googled comas last night and guess what? There are millions of stories about people who didn't come out of them. There are tons of people who end up dying."

Charlie and Mikey sat on their bikes, just looking at me.

"Maybe I'm just really stupid to think she'll wake up."

"No, you're not," Charlie said.

"My grandfather lived," Mikey reminded me.

I turned my head to wipe away my tears before they fell, and there was Casey Cunningham, of all people, coming down the street on her bike. She stopped right in front of us and looked at me. "Are you okay?"

I stood up. "Are you seriously asking if I am okay? With everything you've done to me, do you think I'm okay?"

"You're a jerk." Casey scowled at me and took off on her bike.

Mikey and Charlie kind of stared at me and then each other. I knew they thought I had just blown my one chance with Casey. I didn't care.

Chapter 21

I PICKED MY STUFF UP OFF OF THE STEP. "I better go in now, but I'll see you guys tomorrow."

I greeted the nurses as I passed by their station. Megan came around the desk and stopped me. "Hey, you. Are you okay?"

"I'll be fine." I fake smiled.

She handed me a chocolate bar and a bottle of water. "This always helps me." She smiled.

I climbed up on the bed once again and pulled out the newspaper so I could tell Mrs. McGee about what was going on in the town's politics. I knew she would want to know because even though I detested politics and knew zero about it, I knew that she always thought it was very important to stay on top of current events. But I was tired. I held her hand and closed my eyes.

"Mrs. McGee, today I am going to take a nap with you. I am just so tired."

I'm not sure how much time went by, but something woke me. Or was it a dream? "Mrs. McGee, was that you? Did you just squeeze my hand?"

Seconds felt like hours and minutes felt like days. I breathed slowly and waited with my eyes closed. I felt it again.

"Yes! Thank you!" I threw my arms around her neck and hugged her tight. Jumping up, I ran out to Megan. "Come. Mrs. McGee is waking up."

Megan gently took Mrs. McGee's hand, studied the monitors, and stood there for what seemed like a very long time. "Sweetie, sometimes we want things to happen so badly that we think they have, but I don't think there is any change." She put her hand on my shoulder and looked down at me sadly. "I'm sorry it wasn't what you thought." She brushed my cheek with her hand like a concerned mother would do and headed out the door.

Mom arrived minutes later. "Hi, sweetie. Megan said you thought you felt Mrs. McGee squeeze your hand. I'm sorry she hasn't woken up yet. This has really taken a toll on you. Come. Let's call it a night, and you and I will stop at Lupinacci's Pizza Palace for dinner."

Mom and I said our prayer, kissed Mrs. McGee good night, and went out to the nurses' station.

"I'll be right there, Mom. I just have to get something from her room." Mom stood talking to the nurses while I ducked back in Mrs. McGee's room and whispered to her.

"It's okay, Mrs. McGee. It'll be our secret for now. Tomorrow, I am going to bring you some nail polish, and I'll paint your nails for you so when you wake up you'll look pretty." I kissed her cheek, said "I love you," pretended she said it back, and started to head out.

I turned and looked at her before I opened the door. Nothing was going to change my mind. I had to believe she had just squeezed my hand.

Chapter 22

ARE YOU KIDDING ME? Casey's post today read:

> Who wet the bed until they were eight years
> old, has a dad who left her when she was
> little, and has the hairiest arms in the entire
> world? That's right. Greta Grace Gibson (The
> Try Hard!)

I slammed my hand on the kitchen table. "Seriously, Samantha? How could you tell them all that stuff?" I sank my head into my two hands and shrieked.

Within minutes, there was a text from Charlie that said, "I am going to tell Casey to back off. If she likes me, maybe she'll listen to me."

I texted back, "No, it'll make her meaner. Please don't. Thanks anyway."

Casey was smart. She would leave the post up long enough to cause a stir, but not long enough to chance getting caught once the word got out. I took a screenshot, though. Something inside me told me I just might need it, and so I listened to that voice. *Oh, my gosh! What the heck? Was this ever going to end?*

By the time I got to my locker, it was clear something was going on. I pushed my way through the circle of kids, who were mostly standing with their mouths gaping as they looked at the mounds of shaving cream smeared across my locker. There was a note taped to the locker:

> Thought you might want this for your hairy body.

I could feel my cheeks go hot. My eyes burned with the tears I was holding back from the desperation I felt, and my heart filled with anger like it had never done before.

Suddenly, the kids all seemed to have something better to do and fled the circle.

"Greta Grace, do you know who did this?" I turned to see my social studies teacher, Mr. Lands, standing there, looking down at me. I could barely see his eyes; his heavy eyebrows hovered over them. Tugging on his gray beard, he asked again.

Casey was nowhere in sight. I froze for a minute just to think. *Maybe I should just tell him. But I can't. Then she would start doing stuff outside of school, and that would be even worse.*

"No, Mr. Lands. I have no idea." I turned quickly because I was afraid he would figure me out.

Mr. Lands was shaking his head. "You go tell your guidance counselor about this incident, and I'll have the janitor clean up the mess."

I started down the hall as if I was going to the guidance office and then slipped into the girls' bathroom. *Don't cry, Greta Grace. Don't cry. God, why aren't you answering me?* I closed my eyes and took three deep breaths in and out, while affirming to myself "I am okay," and then walked right past the guidance office and into my class.

I don't have any idea what we were supposed to learn. I wrote my name in bubble letters again and again in my notebook for the entire class. Maybe Casey would get what she wanted. If I kept this up, I would be getting B's, C's and maybe even D's without intentionally trying.

Chapter 23

"GRIEB'S PHARMACY, OPEN UNTIL 5 P.M. Excellent. We made it." Charlie and Mikey followed me down the makeup aisle as if they were walking into some foreign country.

"Hey, Mikey." Charlie nudged him and motioned his head toward Ashley, another girl in our grade who was working at the shop.

Mikey started walking toward the door. "She'll think it's weird I am buying makeup with a girl. I'm out of here."

Charlie agreed. "Yeah, this is kind of weird. We'll be outside."

Mikey walked out the door, with Charlie following behind him. Ashley glanced at them and then continued to stock the shampoo shelves. She wasn't old enough for a job, but her parents owned the shop, so I guess it didn't really matter. She seemed older or, what's the word, more mature than most kids in our grade, anyway.

There were purple, pink and even orange bottles of nail polish lined up in rows and rows. Wasn't there just red? Not too dark, not too pink, not too bright. "Robin Rose." I picked up a bottle. *Mrs. McGee will love this. And look at that! It comes with a free lipstick.*

"This will be lovely on you, dear," the woman, probably Ashley's mom, said, as she put the lipstick in a brown paper bag.

"Thanks." *Did she really think I would wear red lipstick?* I added three pieces of gum for us and paid.

At the corner of Main Street and Saundry Avenue, Charlie and Mikey turned one way, and I went straight.

"Mrs. McGee." I ran into her room with my bag, but the room was empty. I bolted out to Megan. "Where is she?" I pointed to the room.

Megan came around the desk. "Sorry to scare you. I was looking out for you earlier to tell you, but thought maybe you weren't able to get here today. We moved her down the hall to Room 222 because the heating and air conditioning unit isn't working properly in her room."

"Thanks," I said, as I hurried down the hallway.

"Perfect, Mrs. McGee. Room 222, triple digits. Those angels know exactly what they are doing." I spoke to her as though she could hear me. Maybe she could. "Mrs. McGee, I thought something happened to you. They shouldn't scare people like that."

I pulled myself up on her bed again, like I had every other day. "Okay, I only have a little time left after stopping at the store, so I have to work fast." I pulled the polish out of the bag and painted each nail one by one.

"I'm not good at this so you should probably wake up soon so you can do them." I wiped off the polish that had gotten on her skin around her nail and then got up on my knees to put on the lipstick. "Geez, Mrs. McGee. I am definitely not good at this." I grabbed the Kleenex box from beside her bed and wiped off all the lipstick that I put outside her lips. "Okay. Now you look pretty, Mrs. McGee. Really pretty."

Mom walked into the room. "Well, don't you look lovely, Molly. What a thoughtful thing to do, Greta Grace."

"I want her to look pretty when she wakes up." I put the lipstick and nail polish back in the brown bag and stuck it in my backpack.

I turned around to find Mom looking at me with a weird look on her face. Her arms reached out for me to come get a hug. I knew she thought I was becoming "unhinged." That was her word for people who were losing it. I didn't care. I wanted Mrs. McGee to look pretty.

We went through the routine of saying our prayer, kissing her goodbye, telling her we loved her, and then I pretended she said it back. Still, she didn't squeeze my hand. Maybe it was because Mom was here. I would wait until next time.

Chapter 24

A FEW MORE DAYS WENT BY. Her lipstick wore off, but her nails didn't have one single chip. Why would they, when they hadn't even moved? Every day, I swore today was going to be the day and, every day, nothing happened. I had to accept the fact that I obviously made it up when I thought she squeezed my hand. It was just one big fat false alarm.

My heart hurt all the time. I'm not a doctor, but I knew that the longer she stayed like this, the worse it was. I couldn't sleep thinking about it.

One night, I got up from bed and went downstairs for water. Mom was sitting at the computer. She'd pulled up an article entitled "Depression in Young Girls: What you need to know."

"Oh, my gosh, Mom. Aren't I allowed to be sad without you having to google what's wrong with me? I miss

Mrs. McGee, and she may never wake up! Google that and see what it says!" I tore up the stairs, got in bed, and threw the blankets over my head.

"Greta Grace, can we talk?" She knocked softly at my bedroom door.

"What," I said from under the covers.

She came in uninvited and sat on my bed. "I'm sorry if I upset you. You know, I've never been a mom before. I've never had a thirteen-year-old daughter before, and sometimes I just need to make sure that I'm not missing something. I'm doing what good moms do. I would never forgive myself if I did or didn't do something that hurt you. You are just sad, and you're allowed to be sad. I would probably be googling what's wrong with you if you weren't sad. I just needed to be sure. You know me. It's that perfectionist thing coming out. Please come out from under the covers."

I pulled the covers off my head.

She moved closer and hugged me tight. "The roller coaster of emotions probably isn't helped by hormones right now."

"Oh, my gosh, do not even go there." I pulled the covers back over my head.

· · · · ·

I was relieved from having to deal with Casey for the next few days, though. I guess the janitor was really mad about having to clean up all that shaving cream, so he told the principal. The principal called tons of kids into his office. Someone must have hinted that Casey was involved. Maybe it was Samantha, but I doubt it.

Anyway, at 9:10 a.m. on Friday, the school secretary called my classroom.

"Mrs. Keegan, would you please send Greta Grace Gibson to the office? Mr. Long would like to see her."

Everybody turned to look at me. My face was as red as a pepper.

What should I do? Do I tell? Maybe it was time to say something.

As I opened the door to the waiting room to his office, who was there but Casey Cunningham.

"What are you doing here?" she barked at me. "What did you tell them?"

"Nothing."

"Don't even think about it," she warned me.

And I didn't. I went in and said I didn't know anything.

She knew she was on their radar, though, so she backed down. I wasn't sure how long it was going to last, but for now, it was good.

· · · · ·

Unlike other days, I left Charlie and Mikey at Grieb's Pharmacy. They pretended they were going in to buy some candy, but it wasn't really the candy they wanted. Mikey wanted an excuse to talk to Ashley.

So, I walked the short distance left to the hospital and then double-stepped it up the thirty steps to the front door and met Mrs. McGee's daughter at the elevator. She looked super-skinny today. Maybe she hated the hospital food too because she looked like she hadn't eaten since Mrs. McGee came in here. Mom would probably google it to see if something was wrong with her.

"It's me, Mrs. McGee." I propped myself on her bed and pulled out the chocolate chip muffin I had left over from lunch. "I have something to show you."

I started showing her lots of old pictures that Mom and I were looking through the night before. I brought lots of pictures of me and her. I started laughing at all the funny ones.

"Mrs. McGee!" I threw my arms around her and clung to her like a two-year-old who had just found a lost teddy bear.

She squeezed my hand again, and her blue eyes opened up. They were so blue! Maybe they had gotten bluer from being closed for so long, but they were open!

I ran to the nurse's station and got Megan, who called the doctor. I called Mom, who was already on her way.

"Well, Molly," the doctor said after some examining, "you sure are a fighter. Glad to see you found your way back to us."

Mrs. McGee looked at me and smiled. She and I both knew she would not leave me. Megan caught my eye and winked.

Chapter 25

"HEY, GRETA GRACE, I'm thinking of going to that party Saturday night. Do you want to come with me?" Charlie was asking me for a date. It was my dream come true. But I couldn't.

"Uh, no. I distinctly remember hearing them say, 'Do not invite Greta Grace.' I don't want to go anyway. It's okay." But it wasn't okay.

Why would he even want to go to a party with a bunch of people who were torturing me? Grabbing my lunch bag, I snuck out the back cafeteria door. I couldn't pretend for one more minute that I wasn't bothered. Maybe I was starting to crack or, even worse, become unhinged. I went into the girls' bathroom and sat in the stall, eating my sandwich.

"Hey! Come out of there." I could hear Casey's voice on the other side of the stall, and I could see another pair of shoes belonging to whoever was with her. I didn't know whose they were. I just knew they didn't belong to Samantha.

"Get out of there!" She pounded on the door.

Staying silent, I prayed and prayed. "Angels, God, Grandma, please help me. Please, please, help me."

"Girls, can I help?" Mrs. Litchfield, the oldest teacher in our school, popped in just in time.

"Uh, no. We were just worried that Greta Grace was stuck in there. That's all."

"Greta Grace, dear. Are you okay in there?"

The girls walked out.

"Yeah, I'm fine. I just wasn't feeling well." I quickly washed my hands and darted past her before she could see my shaking knees and get a glance at the terror in my eyes.

What was I going to do? This thing with Casey was getting way, way out of control. Maybe it really was time to tell.

I thought about it the whole way to the hospital with Charlie and Mikey. In fact, I thought so hard about it, I almost stepped out in front of a car. One minute I was walking along and the next minute, Charlie was screaming my name and yanking my arm. Not my finest moment!

Anyway, I decided not to say anything to Mrs. McGee. If it upset her and made her sick again, I'd never forgive myself.

I said goodbye to the boys and pulled open the heavy doors to the hospital.

"Brilliant news for you, Greta Grace." Megan came out around the desk as I walked down the corridor to Mrs. McGee's room. "Mrs. McGee is doing really well. Her family is in there with her now."

Grr. Why did I hate it so much when they referred to everyone else as her family?

As I entered Mrs. McGee's room, I flew across it and hugged her. I felt so relieved. "I thought you might die. I was so scared."

"I could never leave my Greta Grace. We'll be back to weeding that garden in no time."

Chapter 26

THE BUS WAS JUST TAKING OFF when it stopped again for me, and the door opened. I squeezed myself into my now permanent seat next to Charlie and Mikey.

"Guess what?" I said. "Mrs. McGee is awake and doing great. She'll be home in no time. The doctor said she's one of the lucky ones. Those are the people who remember what happened and can do the same things they did before they went into a coma. Isn't that awesome?"

Charlie beamed. "I have more good news," he said. His eyes brightened like he had just won the top prize from the yearly school raffle. "Casey is going to back off from now on."

"Are you serious? How do you know that? Are you sure?"

"Yep. I talked to her at the party, and she said she would."

"Wow! That's awesome. This might just be the best day ever. How was the party?"

Wait, he talked to her at the party? Why would he talk to her after what she did to me? Geez, you can't trust anybody these days.

"It was stupid. You didn't miss anything," Charlie said.

"Not stupid for me though," Mikey chimed in. "I got to hang out with Ashley, and guess what? She actually likes me."

Just then, the bell rang for class. "Gotta get to Mr. Beard's room. I'll see you seventh period," said Charlie. With that, he and Mikey took off for class.

I felt like I could breathe this morning. Mrs. McGee was going to be fine, and just maybe Casey would stand by her word to Charlie.

Or maybe not.

Lined up across the hallway were Casey and her group. Samantha, like always, was standing slightly off to the side.

Shoot! Shoot! I thought to myself.

"Greta Grace, going somewhere?" The girls linked arms, blocking the hallway. I rolled my eyes and turned to walk in the other direction.

"Wait, Greta Grace, we have something to show you. Samantha, show her your phone." Casey smirked while Samantha fumbled through her bag for it. Casey took the phone from her and scrolled through the pictures. She held up a picture of Mikey and Ashley hanging out together.

"That's what you wanted to show me? Who cares?"

"Oh, sorry. Wrong picture. Samantha, show her the other one." She handed the phone back to Samantha. Before I knew it, Samantha held the phone up and there in my face was a picture of Casey and Charlie kissing! It felt like my heart was going to explode into a trillion little pieces. No, make that a gazillion pieces. Charlie and Casey were kissing!

"Looks like your boyfriend was having fun at the party without you. Oh, and look, wasn't it so nice of your best friend to want to get the photos for you?" Casey stood there smirking.

I dropped my backpack and lacrosse bag to get a better look at the picture and then glared at Samantha. *How could she?*

I could feel my cheeks burn as red as Dorothy's ruby slippers, and my voice rumbled like a terrible thunderstorm. "He's not my boyfriend, so he can kiss whoever he wants, and for sure, Samantha is not my best friend." I gathered my stuff and turned to walk the long way around the building.

Chapter 27

"WAIT, GRETA GRACE, WAIT. It's not what it seems." Samantha, for the first time in forever, opened her mouth.

I stopped and walked back over and stood in front of Samantha and the fifteen or twenty other people who had swarmed around to watch.

I stepped in close to her face. "You spent all this time helping her make life miserable for me? What happened to you? You were my *best* friend. Get. Out. Of. My. Way. Samantha."

I turned back around. "And you," I screamed as I pointed to Casey. "You are nothing but a bully who nobody likes. People are only friends with you so you won't bully them! You're the loser, not me."

I walked straight through their circle. Glancing back at them over my shoulder, they all just stood there, watching me walk away.

Running after me, Samantha begged, "Greta Grace, please, I'm sorry."

I turned and roared, "Sorry. You say sorry and that's supposed to make it all better. Don't ever, ever, talk to me again. *Ever!*"

Everybody in the surrounding classrooms came out to see what all the commotion was about.

"Hey, Greta Grace. Where are you going? I thought you had math this period." Charlie came around the corner.

"Get out of my way. Casey is down the hall. Looks like that party wasn't so stupid after all." Fury... Rage... Hurt... steamed out of every cell in my body.

I breezed past him like he was yesterday's news. No eye contact. No pause. No nothing.

"GG, wait! Let me explain!" he yelled after me.

With my back to him as I continued to walk away, I yelled back, "There's nothing to explain. Go away."

"C'mon. Listen to me!"

But I was already around the corner and in the nurse's room. Yes. Today, I, Greta Grace Gibson, the kid with 100% attendance for the last three years, was going to say I puked and had to go home. It wasn't such a lie because I felt like I was going to throw up at any moment. I needed to get out of here where there was no Casey. No Samantha. No Charlie.

The nurse called Mom to come pick me up.

"Hey, sweetie. Not feeling well today?" Mom's smile quickly faded when she saw me.

I gathered my things, stormed outside, and burst into tears. "I hate my life. I hate school. I hate Casey. I hate Samantha, and I hate Charlie."

"What in the world do you mean, Greta Grace?" She parked the car, and as we approached the house, she threw her arm around me and led me inside as if she was leading a wounded player off a field.

"Look." I opened my laptop and pulled up all the screenshots I had from Casey and her group.

Go die. No one wants you here.
TRY HARD!

A picture of my locker where they used red lipstick to write "LOOOOOOSER. TRY HARD!"

A picture of a hairy gorilla with my name above it.

Tons of ads for shaving cream and razors.

But of course, the worst of it was the memory I had of the picture of Casey and Charlie kissing!

"Greta Grace! Why didn't you tell me? Does anyone at school know?"

"No, I didn't tell you because I knew you would go to the school, and I thought that would make it worse, so I pretended it had stopped."

"I'm sorry, Greta Grace, that you didn't feel like you could tell me. I wish you hadn't felt like you needed to go through this alone. Stretch yourself out there on the couch with that blanket and have a little nap. I am going to run out to the shop and pick up a few things for dinner. You've been through a lot. You must be exhausted. I won't be long."

With that, Mom put her lipstick on, picked up her purse and keys, then left, locking the door behind her.

I was exhausted. I tucked myself under the blanket and closed my eyes. On days like this, I wished I would never wake up.

I started to cry. *How could Charlie do that? How could I have been so wrong about him?*

Chapter 28

I KNEW WHEN SCHOOL ENDED because the texts from Charlie started flying in.

> **GG, call me.**
>
> *(I ignored it.)*
>
> **At baseball practice. Text you after.**
>
> *(I ignored it.)*
>
> **Practice is over. Call me.**
>
> *(I ignored it.)*
>
> *(Incoming call)*
>
> *(End call.)*
>
> *(Incoming call)*
>
> *(End call.)*

Then came the next set of texts, this time from Samantha.

Greta Grace, I am so sorry. Sorry
about everything.

(I ignored it.)

Greta Grace, don't blame Charlie.
I'm sorry.

(I ignored it.)

Let me explain.

(I ignored it.)

"Are you okay?" Mom came in and watched me as she put away a quart of milk. *Hmm. We have lots of milk, and she said we needed dinner.*

"How could I have been so stupid, Mom? I thought Charlie actually liked me. I mean, *liked* me. I wish I didn't have to go to school again tomorrow morning. In fact, I refuse to go. I'm not going."

"How about I pick you up early from school next week when Mrs. McGee is coming home? I think she would love that and so would I." She smiled, but I could tell she was still worried, or sad, or maybe both.

"Can I?" I felt a tinge of happiness.

"Yes. Her daughter is going to pick her up and is going to stay with her. Once she is sure all is well, she'll head back home to Massachusetts."

"I'm sorry I didn't trust you."

"I understand you were scared. Everything I do is out of love. I would give up my last breath if it meant saving you from pain. I know you are strong and resilient, but that doesn't make any of this easy. I guess one day we'll see this as a great opportunity to learn about forgiveness."

"Forgiveness?! I can't see that happening in this lifetime."

"I hear you. If I were you, it would be impossible for me to even think of it too right now. It's too raw, too fresh. But one day down the road, you'll see that by forgiving, you free yourself, not the person who did something to you. It's kind of like a gift to yourself. Let's see. How do I explain this? When you think of Casey and Samantha right now, you feel lots of anger and hatred, right?"

"Yep."

"So, without forgiveness, those feelings never go away. Even twenty years from now, you'll feel the anger. That's a lot of power to give to someone, don't you think?"

"Yes..."

"You'll need time before this comes easily."

"And then what?"

"Then, eventually, you will feel willing to see things differently. After that, you can let it go and decide from a more peaceful place what role, if any, Casey, Samantha and Charlie will have in your life. But there is no rush, Greta Grace. No rush at all."

"I am positive that will not happen in this lifetime." I got up off the couch and went to make us some hot chocolate.

"How about we bake some fresh bread and finish up those curtains Mrs. McGee started. I picked them up and brought home. I think that would be a nice surprise for her to come home to."

"Great idea," I said. Mom came over and hugged me tightly. "Hang in there, Greta Grace, and trust that God and your angels will always make sure you are okay."

"Really? It didn't feel like God, my angels or anything was looking out for me when all of this was going on."

"Perhaps you were too afraid to trust the guidance God sent you. That happens sometimes." Mom spread out the curtain fabric on the table.

"Wait." I just figured out what she meant. "Oh, my gosh! All these things that have been happening the past few months... Do you mean that when you asked all those times about Casey, that might have been God trying to send me help? Or when Casey asked if I was okay, was that God's way of helping? When Mr. Lands sent me to guidance, was that help? When Mrs. Litchfield came into the bathroom? When the principal called me down? Oh, my gosh! I didn't think that was all help from God. I didn't trust it. I was just so afraid of it getting worse."

"God's will for you is your happiness, always. Just keep trusting that. Believe me, you will have many opportunities for that in your life."

"I am really glad you're my mom." I wanted her to know that.

"And, I'm really glad you're my daughter." She smiled. Then, the texts started again... It was Charlie.

Hey.

Mom looked at me and shrugged. "Maybe the boy deserves two minutes?"

I'll talk to you tomorrow.
I'm busy right now.

Okay.

"Mom, before I even think about forgiving Samantha and Charlie and Casey and everyone else, which by the way won't happen for a very, very long time, are you sure this stuff you and Mrs. McGee teach isn't old-fashioned or outdated? Between you and her, I hear all this stuff about angels, visualization, divine guidance, peace, forgiveness and love, but I mean, no offense, but you guys are kind of old. Samantha told me I was getting weird with this stuff."

Mom laughed. "Greta Grace, they are the laws of the universe. They will be the same eighty years from now. You, my sweet, sweet girl, will turn around and teach them to your own kids and grandkids, just as Mrs. McGee and I have taught them to you. I promise you can rely on them. Samantha thinks it's weird because sometimes it's hard to accept what you don't understand. Maybe someday she'll understand and maybe she won't, and either way is fine."

"Yeah, I know. I think it's time though for me to start doing yoga and meditating again. Life always seems easier when I do." But I also knew the very first thing I was going to do when I saw Charlie next was to give him back his stupid sweatshirt. I had absolutely no use for that anymore.

Mom nodded. "Yes, I've missed my girl at yoga. I also realize you have a lot going on with friends, school, lacrosse and Mrs. McGee. It's okay, though, you can just pick up from where you left off."

Chapter 29

I WALKED THE ENTIRE WAY TO SCHOOL. The breeze felt refreshing as it blew against my face and hair. I made it into the building just in time.

"Hey." Charlie was standing at my locker, waiting for me when I got there. It made me feel sad seeing him there. I also felt like a crack was running straight from the top of my heart to the bottom of it, but I was still mad at him.

"Hey." I started loading up my locker. "You can do whatever you want," I said. "It's not like we like each other, except for friends. So really, you can kiss whoever you want." I shrugged like I couldn't care less. I'd become quite the actress. I pulled his sweatshirt out of my backpack and handed it to him.

Charlie looked sad, but he took the shirt and stuffed it in his backpack. "Casey said if I played this stupid kissing game, she would leave you alone forever. Then she found out that I would never like her, so she changed her mind. I actually did it to try to help you."

"Well, you could have told me that right after the party."

"But it was just a stupid game. To me, it was like kissing my cat. It was, like, a second long, and it was just stupid." He just stood there, looking at me. "I just thought... I guess I just thought you knew I liked you." He looked at me, then at the floor, down the hall, and finally back at me. Uncomfortable was written all over his face.

Is he saying he likes me as a friend or more than a friend?

I was just thinking of what I wanted to say back when he blurted out, "Hey, what's going on over there?"

Charlie pointed to a group of girls. As usual, it was Casey's posse, but there was something different about it. They were clearly angry. Heads were shaking, hands were on hips, and Casey looked furious!

Everyone walked away, leaving Casey on her own.

"Who knows? Drama for Casey today means a drama-free day for me. This is how it used to be." Except of course, I was looking at Charlie from afar back then, and writing Mrs. Greta Grace Gibson Tierney all over the pages in my notebook!

"Are we good?" He raised his hand for a high five.

"Yeah, we're good." I slapped his hand back.

Chapter 30

"MOM, YOU AREN'T GOING TO BELIEVE THIS!" I grabbed her hand as we walked out of the school for my early pick up. "Everything changed today. Casey didn't say a word to me or even look at me. Her friends seem to have ditched her. What do you think happened?"

Mom just kind of smiled and winked. "Let's just say that when people know better, they do better, Greta Grace."

"But how could they suddenly know better?"

"Well, maybe a little birdie flew in with some divine intervention." She unlocked the car doors, and we hopped in.

"Divine intervention. That means you said something to them? When? How?" I grabbed my seatbelt to buckle up.

She put the keys in the ignition and then turned toward me. "When I went out yesterday, I actually went back to the school. I asked to meet with the principal and all the girls who followed Casey's command, but not Casey. I explained that they were likely very good kids making a bad choice, and they were the only ones who could discourage Casey from being a bully. It was time for them to do things differently or they would not only be in trouble with the school, but we would also see how the police could intervene. Of course, nobody wanted that. Samantha was crying and was the first one to crack, with everyone else quickly deciding to do the same. I'm not sure what consequences the principal dealt out or how he handled Casey because I left."

"Wow, that explains it. Today, in the hallway, they must have told her they weren't following her anymore. She was so mad."

"I'm sure they finally realized how much trouble they could get into by blindly following someone else, which is never, ever, a good idea." Mom turned forward and put the car into drive.

"Wow, Mom. Thank you. Thank you for getting this to stop."

"I love you, Greta Grace. Please know you can always trust me. Always."

"I will. I promise."

When we reached our destination, Mom parked the car, leaned over, and hugged me.

· · · · ·

When we got to Mrs. McGee's house, her daughter's car was parked in front, which meant they were home. I flung open the car door and took off running inside.

"Mrs. McGee!" I ran in and hugged her. I couldn't contain my excitement. Neither could Rudy, who was running around in circles.

"Oh, how nice it is to be home. I have missed this place." Mrs. McGee's daughter walked around, opening up the windows.

"Look what we have for you." Mom pulled out the blue plaid curtains we had finished and went to hang them on Mrs. McGee's curtain rod in her living room.

"They're beautiful. Thank you, you two," she said as she scooped up Rudy to give him some more hugs.

Mrs. McGee was home and everything felt alright.

· · · · ·

I went straight to Mrs. McGee's house after school the next day. She was sitting out under her umbrella at her picnic table doing her crossword puzzle.

"Well, there is my sweet girl. I've already brought out our snack, so come talk with me. Your mom filled me in on what's been going on with Casey and Samantha. I'm sorry, Greta Grace. Looking back now, I can think of a dozen times when you probably wanted to say something but didn't."

"It's okay. You had a lot going on, and I just didn't want to make things worse."

"Greta Grace, you could never make things worse. That's just not possible. Your mom is a wise woman. There was no better person to help you than her. Even though it meant her going to the school, which is what you feared the most, the way she handled it was absolutely perfect. She's guided by her faith in everything she does. It's a beautiful way to live life. She's a great mom and I'm very proud of her."

"You're right. She is a great mom. What ever happened with Dr. Klyne?"

"When I feel a bit stronger, then we'll tackle that test. I know I am fine though, so I am not at all worried."

I actually didn't have it in me to worry for one more minute. I was just going to have to trust God with this one. I was legitimately worn out.

Mom arrived shortly later with a big cheese pizza! My favorite!

· · · · ·

We had barely gotten home when the doorbell rang. I flew to the door. It was Samantha.

"Oh... What do you want?" I pursed my lips, put on my best mean girl look, and folded my arms.

"Please, just give me five minutes, Greta Grace."

Samantha's thin little body, decked out in ripped jean shorts and a tank top, stood in front of me. There was absolutely nothing she could say that would change my mind about her.

"I am so sorry. I was terrified of Casey, so I messed up everything. If you need a way out of this, follow her home. Go to her house."

"Thanks, but no thanks." I shut the door.

"Who was that?" mom yelled out to me as I shut the door.

"Samantha. She came to say sorry or something."

Mom walked into the living room. "I can't even imagine what you have been going through, Greta Grace. Being betrayed by your friend has to be the most painful thing ever."

"It was awful. I don't know that I'll ever like her again. I would never have done that to her."

She grabbed my hand. "Let's go pick up some sandwiches and head to the beach to eat them. It's a beautiful, warm night and I can't think of one thing that would be better than that." And so we did, and it was perfect.

Chapter 31

THERE WERE ONLY A FEW WEEKS LEFT OF SCHOOL. I lay back in the grass with Rudy jumping on and over me while Mrs. McGee sat under an umbrella looking through a cookbook. The sky was bluer than I ever remembered it being. The flowers were so pretty, and the birds were chirping like crazy.

Mom said Mrs. McGee was once again as "strong as an ox." I don't exactly know how strong an ox is, but clearly it's very strong. Her daughter didn't need to live with her anymore.

"Hey there." Charlie and Mikey rode up on their bikes.

I sat up, brushing away the bead of sweat that had run down my forehead, and introduced Charlie and Mikey to Mrs. McGee.

"Come with us. We want to show you something."

"Where? Now?" I jumped up and dusted off the back of my shorts. "You don't mind, Mrs. McGee. Do you?"

"Of course not, Greta Grace. Elizabeth is coming to visit shortly, anyway." Mrs. McGee nodded toward Charlie and winked at me. I couldn't help but smile. I shook my head and looked away before he caught us.

"Wait. Let's get Ashley too. I told her I'd hang out with her today."

Before I knew it, we met Ashley and were in front of a long and narrow dirt road. There was no grass or flowers, just some dead trees scattered around and lots of overgrown shrubs. It felt like a secret part of our town.

There were about fifteen old, beat-up trailers lined up closely to each other with some rusty barbecue grills in between. There was a long piece of rope tied to two trees and clothes were hanging from it. In a big mound of dirt, there were about ten little kids with pails and shovels just digging.

Quietly, we ducked below an old, cracked stone wall. A girl came out of a trailer and sat down with the little kids in the dirt.

"Oh, my gosh! That's Casey!" I watched with my mouth wide open. One by one, the little kids would jump on her and hug her. She'd tickle them to move them off, and the next one would do the same. She was laughing. She was nice. She was fun.

A tall, red-haired woman came out to help with the pack of kids. She looked like Casey, except she had straight hair. Some other ladies came out of some of the other trailers and sat with her at a picnic table, chatting with one another.

"I never even knew this street was here," I whispered to Charlie. "Does she live here?"

"Yeah. This is why Samantha told you to follow her home."

I nodded. "This explains so much."

Mikey chimed in, "Also explains why she gets off the bus five blocks away from her stop."

"Yeah, but that doesn't make anything she did right," Ashley whispered.

Mikey nodded his head in agreement.

"C'mon, let's get out of here." Charlie waved at us all to follow him.

"What the heck? What are you doing here?" Casey started walking up the dirt road as we pulled our bikes out of the bushes. She definitely was not laughing, nice or fun anymore. She was back to her barking, mean, scary voice.

"We were just riding by." I could feel all that fear again that I felt before, except this time it didn't last. I knew right away this time that I would trust God.

"If you tell anyone I live here, I promise you I will make your life miserable." She stood eye to eye with me. Charlie and Mikey got off their bikes and walked over. But I didn't back down.

"In case you forgot, you've already done that to me a thousand times. I won't tell anyone, but it's not because I'm scared of you." I walked back to my bike.

"How do I know you won't?"

"Because I don't live to ruin people's lives. Nobody cares where you live." I threw my leg over the seat of my bike and took off. "C'mon, guys. Let's head to the lake."

Chapter 32

CHARLIE AND MIKEY PULLED OVER at the end of the street, and Charlie said, "Really? After everything she did to you, you're not going to say anything to anybody?"

"Why not? After what she did to you?" Ashley looked at me like I was crazy not to take my chance. "She deserves it. She should get a taste of her own medicine."

"She knows I could if I wanted to. That's enough for her to leave me alone for the rest of my life. I don't want revenge, so I'm just going to let it go."

Ashley scrunched her face up, totally confused.

"Okay, all hands in." I put my fist out.

We all bumped fists to make it official. No one would say anything. That's the way I wanted it.

The lake was packed. The warm sun and slight breeze made it a perfect day. Setting up a spot, I had to laugh as I shared the story of the day I fell in. Yet, *here I was, sitting at the same lake with Charlie. Destiny, if you ask me!*

As I turned my head, I saw Samantha and my old friends were set up across the way.

Charlie saw them. "Uh oh. Do you want to move?"

"No, it's fine." It seemed so long ago that I used to be part of that group. I kind of just sat and watched Samantha for a bit. *Why in the world did she turn on me like that? What was really going on?*

Life seemed to rewind the next day. I was still sitting in my new bus seat with Charlie and Mikey, but I was no longer looking over my shoulder. I went to and from my locker, not expecting any shaving cream or signs or anything. The next day, after coming back from being suspended, Casey passed by me in the hallways like she never knew I existed, and like before, there was a seat at the girls' lunch table for me.

"No thanks," I mumbled as I walked by with my hot lunch of tater tots and what they tried to pass off as a hamburger. Pulling out my chair from what had become my very own table, Mikey, Charlie and Ashley came over, put their trays on the table, and pulled out their chairs.

It was nice to feel normal again. It was nice to feel like I belonged somewhere, and it was the perfect way to start summer. This was one I was ready for.

I planned to spend it mostly sleeping in late, perfecting how to do laundry and even folding fitted sheets, hanging out with my friends, and watching lots of movies with both Mom and Charlie. Oh, and Mom and I have decided to eat really healthy this summer. We are going to do yoga three times a week, and we have joined a meditation that Mrs. McGee is running at the recreation center in town. I'll probably be the only kid there, but Mom keeps saying, "You will thank yourself for the rest of your life, Greta Grace, if you make this a normal routine."

I never really know how to explain what it does for me to my friends, but I like it. I actually do it almost every day on my own. Very proud of myself!

Chapter 33

"MRS. MCGEE, ARE YOU HERE?" I knocked on her door as hard as I could. "Oh, my gosh! Mrs. McGee!" I yelled as I ran to the backyard. "Where are you?"

Taped to her door was a note.

> Greta Grace,
> Be right back. Just at Rudy's checkup.

I sat down on her steps and thought about how happy I was that she was still alive. I closed my eyes and tilted my head toward the sun. I know Mrs. McGee was right when she said the sun was bad for you, but Mom read me a book when I was little that said to imagine ourselves as the rays to the sun, God being the sun and us being the rays. Since then, I always thought about that. I let the sun's light pour into my heart and fill it up. Doing it always made me feel happy. Mrs. McGee could never argue with that.

. . . . .

"Hey, sweet girl," Mrs. McGee called out as Rudy ran over, and I scooped him up and cuddled him on my lap. "How about we take a little walk down to Dairy Queen on this delightful day?"

"No twisting my arm there." Every person who knew me knew DQ was my favorite place in the entire world. Chocolate ice cream with peanut butter cups was my all-time favorite. Mrs. McGee always got her vanilla ice cream with butterscotch topping.

The line for the outdoor service window wrapped around the building. "Wow! Mrs. McGee, we don't have to stay."

"I don't mind, if you don't," she said as she headed to the back of the line. I was caught off guard by Samantha, who was already in line.

She glanced at me and then looked away, probably hoping that I didn't see her see me.

"Hi, Samantha." Part of me never wanted to forgive her, but I had to admit that just a small, itty-bitty piece of me was willing to believe that she really was sorry. Mom and Mrs. McGee always say, "Be willing to see things differently."

"Hi, Greta Grace." She smiled with an apologetic look.

"Line is long. I better go get in it." I continued down the line to meet up with Mrs. McGee. She just put her arm around me and smiled.

Samantha turned around, called my name, and pointed to the time on her phone. I pulled mine out of my pocket and glanced at it. The time read 4:44. That was my favorite trio. I looked up and gave her a half-smile.

"I wonder if that's a sign from the angels that we'll end up friends again." I looked at Mrs. McGee and shrugged.

"You don't have to decide anything today, Greta Grace. You'll find out eventually if she is in your life for a short time or for a lifetime. What about your friend Charlie?" She looked at me and smiled.

"Oh, Mrs. McGee, I hope he's for a lifetime. Mrs. Greta Grace Tierney. Doesn't that sound just perfect!"

"Perfect indeed, Greta Grace. Perfect indeed." Mrs. McGee let out one of her hearty laughs.

"Okay. Well, he didn't ask me to marry him yet, but look, he just sent a text asking me, Ashley and Mikey if we want to go to the summer carnival at school tonight." I held my phone up for her to read the text.

"Sounds like a double date to me." Mrs. McGee winked.

Chapter **34**

THE LIGHTS FROM THE RIDES LIT UP THE SKY, bells rang from the game booths, and the cotton candy and fried dough lines seemed to never end. It amazed me that our school grounds could actually be turned into something like this.

"Hey, let's go on the Ferris wheel." Charlie pointed up to the gondolas, practically touching the clouds. Mike and Ashley agreed immediately.

"Okay," I half-heartedly answered. "I'm just not the best with heights."

"I'll sit with you if you want," Ashley whispered.

"It's okay. I'm sure you want to sit with Mikey, and if I am actually going to agree to do this, I'm at least going to get to sit with Charlie." I laughed nervously.

My stomach was doing flips just standing in line, watching. *Geez, with everything Mom and Mrs. McGee taught me, couldn't they have taught me how to get over my fear of heights? Seriously, I don't actually know if I can get on that ride, and then I'll ruin everything!*

Just then one of their quotes popped into my head, "Don't always believe your thoughts."

Ah! What does that even mean? Oh! Why did they have to choose this ride?

"Next in line!" The operator of the ride gestured to Charlie and me. We got in, and he pulled down the bar to make sure we were secure. I double-checked it, you know, just to be really sure. Then I closed my eyes tight and kept reminding myself not to believe my thoughts.

"You okay, GG?" Charlie laughed.

"I hope so." I laughed a fake laugh while keeping my eyes closed.

"It'll be fine." He put his arm around my shoulder.

I know this should have made me want to jump for joy, but I couldn't. As the ride started to move, I clenched the bar tighter and repeated "Nothing bad is going to happen" over and over.

Charlie grabbed my hand. "It's okay, GG. Nothing bad is going to happen."

He smiled, and then he did it! He leaned in and kissed me on the lips. It was perfect! *Please don't let this ride end. Please don't let this ride end.*

The ride did end, but my romantic evening didn't. Charlie grabbed my hand, and he, Mikey, Ashley and I walked around to find our next ride. Oh, God! The next ride was not only high up, but spun around wildly at the same time. A definite recipe for vomit, sweat and tears. *Seriously... there are so many other rides here besides this.*

"GG, can you handle this?" Ashley asked before we handed our tickets over to the next operator.

"I'll be fine," I told her. I know Mom said to never, ever give into peer pressure, but it's not like I just took a beer from someone. Anyway, it was time to get over this fear. Still, I felt that flipping feeling in my stomach all over again. Ugh!

I can't say much about the ride because even though I had the best intentions, I closed my eyes, prayed and gritted my teeth through the entire thing. Why did I think it would be a good idea to conquer spinning and heights in one night? That just wasn't going to happen.

The perfect night ended. As we were walking out of the gates to our rides home, we walked past Samantha and my old friends. With Charlie holding my hand, I glanced over and caught them all looking at us. Samantha smiled and gave me a thumbs-up. I grinned and went on my way.

Chapter 35

THE NEXT MORNING, while I was pouring a huge bowl of cereal before I plopped myself down in front of Netflix, my phone beeped with a text.

It was from Samantha and said, "Hey! Excited to see you and Charlie last night. Are you guys dating?"

I didn't answer. I wasn't sure why she wanted to know that information. Was she trying to be a good friend again? Did someone ask her to find out? Was she spying for somebody else? Maybe we would be friends one day, but right now I still couldn't trust her.

My circle was small these days since I only hung out with Mikey, Charlie and Ashley, but it was a good circle. I guess it is true when they say quality is much more important than quantity. It would be interesting to see what the next school year would be like. I would find out very quickly because there was only one more week left in the summer.

Mom always says, "Summer is never as long as we think it is." I finally understood what she means by that. It felt like it had just started, and it was already nearly over.

Schedules came out with class assignments and teachers. Texts and postings were flying around as everyone hurried to find out who was with who. Charlie and I had math and science together. You know I was happy about that! Samantha and I were in English together. Not sure how I felt about that... And Mikey, Ashley and I all had PE together. Not sure what Casey had because she didn't post anything. I would be fine if I didn't have anything with her.

We were starting eighth grade, and I was so excited and nervous at the same time. I loved getting ready for school to start. I laid out all of my new school supplies neatly on my desk and matched up outfits with the new clothes Mom and I bought on our shopping spree. I picked my favorite outfit for tomorrow. I wanted to look good when I saw Charlie on the bus in the morning.

It ended up that Casey was in my science class. She sat all by herself. I have to say that, for one minute, I, actually maybe just one-tenth of me, felt sorry for her. She still had that overconfident face, but that loud, gruff voice seemed quiet, like a sad quiet. She looked downright sad.

I shouldn't feel sorry for her. Why should I? She literally ruined my life at one point. I should be mad at her for the rest of eternity. I commanded my mind to not feel bad for her, and I didn't want to think about how her life might be really hard. She obviously didn't do any after-school activities, and she had no life at home after school because she was watching a bunch of little kids.

I thought about my mom being a single mom. Maybe my life could have been like Casey's. Mom only had me to take care of, but her mother had something like five kids. Maybe Mom wouldn't have been able to survive either if there was more than me.

What if we lived in the projects? Would I act a certain way just so people didn't think I was less than them?

I don't know. But maybe.

Wait! Was I starting to forgive her? Was this what Mom meant?

Chapter 36

"Mrs. McGee, your favorite kid in the whole world is here!" I walked into the kitchen to see Mrs. McGee and her granddaughter sitting at the kitchen table; the kid with the long black braids and the pink high-tops. You know, the one who was rude and super-obnoxious when she saw me hiding behind the tree.

"Hello, my sweet girl." Mrs. McGee got up and gave me a big, extra-tight hug. "Have you met Courtney before?"

"We met briefly when you were in the hospital, although I didn't catch her name then." I glanced at her and quickly looked away.

"I figured you and I could show her what life is like here in Fairfield, Connecticut."

"Uh, sure." I lied. I had no intention of "showing her life in Fairfield, Connecticut." *Why didn't Mrs. McGee tell me she was coming? I would have gone straight home if I had known.* "Uh… I better get going, though. I have a ton of homework."

"Are you sure? You haven't had your snack or told me anything about your day."

"Yeah, I'm sure. I have a big test tomorrow so I better get studying for that."

She followed me to the door. "Greta Grace, I'm sorry to spring this on you. My daughter called me yesterday in a panic because apparently Courtney started hanging out with a particular group of kids and her mother wants to separate her from them. I meant to call you and your mom last night, but I fell asleep early, and then you were in school all day. I'm sorry about that."

I couldn't stand Mrs. McGee feeling bad. "It's totally fine. It would be terrible if she started doing bad stuff with troublemakers."

"I love you, my sweet girl. I really do. You know how I always say that God puts people into our lives for a reason? Well, I'm pretty sure He needs me, and maybe even you, to be in her life right now. Not for one second does that mean that you are being replaced or loved less or that I won't look forward to you coming here every single day."

"I know. It's fine." I hugged her tight, grabbed my backpack, and headed out the door.

I wanted it to be fine. It should be fine, and I didn't want Mrs. McGee to feel bad, but like, seriously? How could things possibly be normal with her here?

Mom and I went to Lupinacci's Pizza again for dinner. It was always Mom's pick-me-up kind of place.

"So, tell me about Courtney. Mrs. McGee called me today to say that she was arriving."

"She's fine. It's fine. If it's not fine, then I guess I can't visit Mrs. McGee for this school year. That's all."

"I don't think that would make you happy, do you? I know this is difficult because it's always been just you and Mrs. McGee. You two are quite the duo. She loves you like you are her very own and nothing will ever change that." Mom ate a slice of pizza. "I'm sure this might be a little hard for her too. She's probably worried about Courtney and the choices she's been making. It might also be a little daunting for Courtney. I imagine leaving your family, friends and school could be difficult. Maybe you should give her a chance."

"Whatever. You don't get it." I suddenly lost my appetite.

"Get what?"

"It's weird. She changes everything. It's not going to be fine. It's going to be terrible."

"I understand where you are coming from. I promise I do. It probably feels like she moved right into your own home, but you get to choose how this whole thing plays out."

No, I don't. If I got to choose, I'd choose she wasn't here. "Whatever," I said. "I'm done. Can we go?"

It was a silent car ride home. I was mad at Courtney for coming here. I was mad at her mother, who obviously couldn't raise her right. I was mad at Mom for having an ounce of sympathy for Courtney, and yes, I was mad at Mrs. McGee. There. I said it. I was ticked off with Mrs. McGee.

Chapter 37

MOM ALWAYS SAYS that women need to take care of them-
selves. Okay, I may not be a mature, motherly woman, but
I decided I needed a break. I didn't go to Mrs. McGee's
house for the next few days. We FaceTimed every day,
but we never talked about Courtney.

I missed Mrs. McGee. I missed her a lot! I missed
hanging out at her house, but I felt like going there
would be torturing myself. If she missed me enough,
maybe she would send Courtney home—and if not,
then maybe not visiting was going to be my new norm,
and I should just get used to it. Anyway, soccer would
start soon and with eighth grade also came tons of
homework. There would be lots to keep me occupied,
including Charlie. He and I were doing just fine!

For now, I would just start my day and figure everything else out later. The bus pulled up, and I hopped on.

"Hey, GG!" Charlie called out. His voice still made me tingle.

"Hey!" I said as I sat next to him. Last week, he, Mikey, Ashley and I decided we would get two seats, one in front of the other.

The bus was just about to pull off when Courtney got on. Once again, she had her hair in those long black braids. I didn't want to admit it, but she had a cool outfit on and her makeup looked perfect.

"Hey, who's the new girl?" Charlie nodded her way.

"She's Mrs. McGee's granddaughter. She moved here from Massachusetts about a week ago, but she must have just gotten registered for school."

"Then you probably know her, right? I mean, considering you hang out there all the time."

"I haven't really been there that much since she came."

Charlie looked at me. "That stinks. I would have thought you two would have become friends."

I got quiet. He kind of sounded like Mom, but seriously, why did I always have to be the one to do the right thing?

I also hated that Courtney wasn't acting like that sarcastic, crazy girl I saw when she was running around tossing Mrs. McGee's hat in the air. She sat in a seat and started scrolling through her phone.

Just then, Casey got on the bus and sat beside her.

"Oh, my gosh." I whispered to Charlie, Ashley and Mikey. "Look who is sitting next to Courtney."

"Wait, explain to me why you guys aren't already friends. Is she, like, really mean or something?" Ashley wanted the scoop on her.

I looked at them blankly. I actually didn't have one good reason for not speaking to her even once since she got here. And now, what if she became a target of Casey's? If nothing else, I should have warned her.

I decided I would stop by Mrs. McGee's after school to see her and that I would also warn Courtney about Casey. *It was time to man up or woman up. What's that saying again?*

Chapter 38

"HEY, COURTNEY." I paused after we got off the bus. "Are you going home now?"

"Not home to Massachusetts, but home to my grandmother's. Why?"

"Because I thought I'd stop by and see her." I started walking with her.

"Yeah, okay. It was kind of mean of you to just stop coming by anyway."

"Mean of me? Me? The person you should worry about being mean is Casey. Seriously, she's the mean one. You can ask anybody."

"She's been nothing but nice to me." Courtney shrugged. "You'll be happy to know I'm going home Friday for the weekend. In fact, I'm going to go home every weekend."

She really thought I was mean. "I'm not glad you're leaving every weekend," I told her. "Okay. Well, truthfully, part of me is probably glad you are since I've never had to share Mrs. McGee before, but I'm still sorry that I've been a bit of a jerk."

"A bit of a jerk? You've been a total jerk."

"Tell me what you really think," I laughed.

"You picked the wrong day to come over, though, because I invited Casey over today. My grandmother said I could invite anyone I thought would make a good friend, so I invited her."

I thought this over. "I doubt she can come. She takes care of a bunch of kids after school."

"Yeah, well, she said her mom was off this week, so she could probably come. That's if she got a ride."

We walked into Mrs. McGee's house to the smell of oatmeal cookies baking in the oven. I hugged her tight. It was good to be back. I decided I didn't want to be the cause of Mrs. McGee feeling bad anymore. We sat around the living room coffee table eating cookies, talking about classes, teachers, the cafeteria food, and every other school detail. I realized Courtney was funny. She was witty and sarcastic and kind of fun to be around. It had to feel good for Mrs. McGee to have the two of us getting along and for me to have stopped acting like a spoiled brat.

The doorbell rang.

"Oh, Grandma. I forgot to tell you. I invited a friend over today. That must be her."

"Terrific, dear. Greta Grace, if she is from your grade you must know her too."

Before I could even answer, Casey was in the doorway. Mrs. McGee's eyes grew wide as she looked at Casey and then me. Casey's eyes grew wide as she looked at me and then Mrs. McGee. Clearly, she had no idea we were connected to Courtney. Courtney dragged Casey into the kitchen to get a cookie.

Mrs. McGee said, "Greta Grace, I'm sorry. I didn't know she meant Casey. This must be terrible for you."

"It's fine. Even though I'll probably never be friends with Casey, I think I have sort of forgiven her. It's all kind of how you said it would be."

She threw her arms around me and gave me a huge hug. "I love my sweet girl. What would I do without you?" I was happy to hear that.

Casey and Courtney were sitting at the kitchen table. It was awkward. Even though I didn't hate Casey like I used to, this was just weird. I didn't know what I should do, so I started helping Mrs. McGee wash some dishes.

"Are you kidding me, Greta Grace? We won't bite. Come sit down." Courtney pulled her feet off the chair next to her.

"I don't understand why you invited me. Are you two going to ambush me or something?" Casey looked a little nervous as she looked at Courtney and me.

"What? Why would we do that?" Courtney looked at her like she was crazy.

"I'm sure Greta Grace told you." Casey looked directly at me.

"Um... No, I didn't." I shook my head.

"Okay, then. Forget it." Casey picked up another cookie.

"Hey, why don't you two show me where that Dairy Queen is?" Courtney stood up and started counting some dollar bills she pulled out of her pocket. She couldn't have cared less about what went down between Casey and me.

Within the first couple of weeks, Courtney had like five hundred friends, including Samantha. She was just like that. She talked to everyone, including the boys, and everyone loved her. Unlike me, she was a terrific flirt. As long as she stayed away from Charlie, it didn't matter. She didn't care a whole lot about schoolwork, but she did enough to get by.

"Hey, GG." Charlie met me at my locker after school. "How about going roller skating Saturday night?"

"Sounds great! Let's ask Ashley and Mikey too."

Courtney walked up. "And what are you two talking about?" *How did she so comfortably make herself part of conversations? I wish I could do that.*

"About roller skating this weekend. Too bad you go home on the weekends or you could have come." I turned to finish getting everything out of my locker.

"Actually, I think my parents would be fine with me staying here for the weekend, especially since they value good friends. I'll check with them. Maybe we could get a group of people. That would be kind of weird if I just went with you guys."

I hesitated then, but I said, "Sure, why not? That might be fun."

"Okay. You can come to my grandmother's early on Saturday, and we can get ready there. We'll figure out the exact plans later. Gotta run! I have to get to English." She took off.

Chapter 39

"MOM, I'M GOING OVER TO MRS. MCGEE'S to get ready to go roller skating tonight. Can you pick me up at 10:30 p.m. from the rink?" I grabbed the bag that I had packed my clothes in to wear later.

"Of course. You seem to like Courtney these days. That's nice."

"Yeah, she's actually a lot different from the first time I met her." I gave her a big hug and headed out the door. I was feeling kind of bad. Mom and I used to have movie nights on Saturday nights when I didn't have a life, which was right up until pretty recently.

I hung out with Mrs. McGee for a bit and then went upstairs. Courtney had just started blow-drying her long black hair. It was as shiny as a pair of polished black shoes. *Why couldn't I have gotten hair like that?* She had a pair of cut-off jean shorts on and a red halter top that showed off most of her stomach, her really flat stomach.

"I hate my outfit." I was embarrassed to pull my plain white T-shirt and striped blue and white shorts out of my bag. I looked like a little kid next to Courtney.

"You can borrow some of my stuff. Go ahead in my closet and pick out anything you want. We're probably the same size." Courtney was putting on eyeliner and mascara, which was something else I knew nothing about.

"Thanks. Maybe next time. I'll just wear this for today." As desperate as I was not to wear my outfit, Mom would kill me if she saw me show up with shorts that short and half of a shirt. And Mrs. McGee? Her head would roll if I walked down in that. But I wanted to. I really, really wanted to.

"Courtney Marie Murphy, does my daughter really let you leave the house looking like that?" Mrs. McGee put her hands on her hips and shook her head in disbelief. "Do you not have a respectable outfit like Greta Grace to wear?"

Courtney laughed. "Grandma, it's what everyone wears. You are just behind the times." *So am I. I should have just borrowed her outfit.*

Mom took us to the rink and dropped us off. I would guess half of the grade was there. Casey was not, but I wasn't surprised. She was probably babysitting.

"Courtney, come here."

"Courtney, look at this."

"Courtney, sit here."

Everywhere I turned, someone was begging for her attention. She had only been in the school for a few weeks. How did she do that?

"C'mon, GG. Let's skate." Charlie came over and grabbed my hand. In an instant, I no longer cared.

As we came around from the first lap, Samantha walked in and immediately waved Courtney off the rink. They gave each other big hugs, like they hadn't seen each other in years. Courtney took off her skates, threw on her sneakers, linked arms with Samantha, and off they went to the girls' bathroom. That usually meant that someone wanted to fix her hair or check her makeup or something like that. They had the exact same sneakers on. I mean, like the exact same color, make and everything.

By the time we had done another couple of laps, Courtney and Samantha had come up to the plexiglass surrounding the rink. Since Samantha didn't feel like skating, she and Courtney just hung out. Within minutes, there was a swarm of other kids around them.

"Hey, what's up?" I asked as we skated over and opened the gate to meet them.

"Next weekend," started Courtney, "I have to go home to Massachusetts on Saturday. So let's plan for pizza on Friday night."

Everyone agreed. More plans for next weekend. Yay!

Chapter 40

"HI, MRS. MCGEE. Do I smell chocolate chip muffins?" I went over and gave her a hug.

"Yes, my sweet girl, just for you."

Courtney had been meeting Casey at the playground every day after school to hang out with her while she watched her siblings. It was working out nicely for me and Mrs. McGee.

"Do you think it's a good idea for Courtney to be hanging out with Casey? I have to admit, it has me a little worried." Mrs. McGee looked concerned, a look that I hadn't seen in a long time.

"It's fine, Mrs. McGee. She's a lot more normal now. As soon as she found out that we knew where she lived, things changed."

"Greta Grace, I know Courtney moving here couldn't have been easy for you. Thank you for being such a good sport about it."

"Actually, I wasn't a good sport at all. Even though I know everything happens for a reason, I just couldn't stop being upset over it. I'm sorry."

"No apology needed, my sweet girl. I know that it's just been us for a very long time. Change can be challenging."

When I got home that day, Mom had made my favorite dinner and my all-time favorite dessert, a strawberry shortcake.

"I thought it was time for a girls' night," she said as she laid out roast beef, mashed potatoes, peas, gravy and dinner rolls on the table. "I was thinking today, Greta Grace. It's been too long since we did this. Now, catch me up with the details of your life."

"Okay. Where do I start? Courtney. I like Courtney. Actually, the whole world likes Courtney. Charlie, I really, really like him. He's just nice, normal. You know what I mean?"

Mom smiled and nodded her head.

I was just getting started. "Samantha. Samantha is part of our group because Courtney became friends with her. But it's fine. Samantha and I kind of just started talking again. It's almost like things are slowly getting back to normal. Actually, she's going to come over here Friday before we go for pizza with everyone and then she'll sleep over. Casey. Believe it or not, Casey is part of our group. She's actually a pretty quiet person. She doesn't say a lot, but she doesn't cause trouble or anything either. Mikey? He and Ashley are still dating. You know them. They're cool people. But Mom, I need to go shopping. My clothes look like they belong to a third or fourth grader. Seriously, I do."

Mom laughed. "Go shopping. I just don't want to see any body parts hanging out that shouldn't be. If you want to invite a couple of friends, I can drop you off at the mall on Thursday."

"You really are the best mom. I think I might actually ask Samantha to come with me and Ashley." I got up and hugged her.

"Now I'm heading off to yoga. Would you like to come? Tonight is hot yoga."

"Of course I would! I'll go get ready."

· · · · ·

The week flew by, and Thursday finally came. Ashley and Samantha got off the bus with me. Casey and Courtney headed off in the opposite direction so they could go babysit Casey's siblings. We visited with Mrs. McGee, and then Mom came and got us and dropped us off at the mall. We ended up in our favorite store and grabbed stacks of clothes to try on. We would each try on an outfit and then come out to see what the other ones thought about it.

"Greta Grace, that is perfect!" Samantha gave me two thumbs up as I stepped out with a pair of white shorts and a pink flouncy halter top I would wear Friday night. The shorts were shorter than all my other shorts, but still, nothing was hanging out, so it would pass Mom's test. Ashley settled on the same shorts in denim, but

Samantha didn't want any. She said her sister had lots of stuff to lend her.

"Okay, you guys come to my house tomorrow to get ready, and then my mom will drop us off. If you guys want to sleep over, you can. Just bring your stuff when you come to get ready." Samantha nodded her head in agreement.

Ashley shook her head. "My crazy parents don't allow sleepovers, but I'll come get ready with you guys."

"With five siblings, people in my house won't even know I'm missing," Samantha laughed.

"Hey, Samantha. Mom said your house is for sale?"

We grabbed our bags.

"Let's get going," she said. She blushed and looked away. That always meant she didn't want to talk about something.

Chapter 41

THERE WERE THREE BLOW-DRYERS GOING when Mom poked her head into my room on Friday. She smiled and closed the door again.

"Let me put some eyeliner and mascara on you, Greta Grace." Samantha pulled out a small bag with the essentials, and when she was done, she stood back and admired me. "That's perfect. You look beautiful."

I went and stood in front of the full-length mirror on the back of my door. I felt very grown up and was excited to see Charlie!

The three of us jumped into the car, and Mom dropped us off in town. We figured we'd walk around a bit before meeting everyone for pizza.

"Greta Grace." Samantha stood beside me as I looked at the new fall clothes in the window of one of the shops.

"Yeah?" I was trying to read the price of one of the shirts.

"I'm really, really sorry about the whole Casey thing. I really am. There's nothing I can say that would make it okay. I was petrified of Casey, and I couldn't give my parents one more thing to worry about, so I bailed on you, and I am so, so, so sorry. I don't know how I even turned into that person who was so awful to you. I didn't let myself think about it, because when I did, I always went to pick up the phone to call you, especially after you left the message about the lake. You know that quote your mom has on your fridge? The one that says 'When you know better, you do better?'"

"Yep. It's still there."

"Well, I know better now. I would never, ever do anything like that again to you or anyone."

"Why, though?" I really wondered why she turned on me.

"I'll explain later, but I am sorry."

I put my hand up for our handshake. "We're good."

"Hey, wait a minute. You can't do that without me." Ashley stuck her hand in the middle to join in. "Teach me! I want to be part of it."

"Next time. It takes a long time to learn. C'mon, let's head to the pizza place. I'm starving." I linked arms with both girls, and we headed down the road.

We arrived at the pizza place before anyone else and pushed tables together to make room for everybody.

"Hey, guys!" Courtney and Casey walked in soon after we got there. Of course, Courtney looked like she was off the cover of a magazine, but Casey—Casey looked like we had never seen before. Her wiry, red ringlets were blown into a smooth, super straight look and she had on mascara and lip gloss. She was stunning. They walked over to the two tables we had pushed together and sat down. Two minutes later, Charlie and Mikey arrived. Charlie sat down next to Courtney while Mikey went and sat down next to Ashley, who tossed a straw at Charlie.

"Charlie, what are you doing?" she asked him. "You're supposed to sit next to Greta Grace."

He turned red and just laughed.

I turned red and laughed too. Maybe we weren't so good at this dating thing.

I needed somebody's opinion, so when Samantha and I got back to my house, I had to say something. "Samantha, do you think it's weird that Charlie didn't sit next to me at the pizza place?" I lathered my face with soap to take off the makeup.

"I don't know." Samantha paused, brushing her teeth. "Maybe he didn't think and just grabbed the first seat he saw."

"I hope it's not because he stopped liking me."

"Seriously, I wouldn't worry about it. Guys just don't think." She threw her curly hair into a high bun on her head and jumped into bed.

"Guess you're right. Good night."

Chapter 42

MONDAY MORNING CAME SOONER THAN I WANTED. Samantha came by, and we grabbed Courtney from Mrs. McGee's house and headed off to the bus. We took our regular seats.

"Hey, GG. Look what I got for you." Charlie handed me a pack of my favorite gum.

"Thanks!" I gave him a hug and then glanced over at Samantha as if to tell her she was right. There was nothing to worry about.

"Okay, you guys." Courtney addressed the group. "What's up this weekend? It's almost Halloween, so why don't we have a Halloween party? Greta Grace, do you think my grandmother would let us have one?"

"Maybe. Probably." I had no idea.

"Okay. Greta Grace, you ask her after school. You guys hold tight, and we'll let you know. In the meantime, think of some costumes."

Truthfully, I hated Halloween. I hated dressing up. I hated the decorations. I pretty much hated everything about it.

"Charlie, come here." Courtney had gotten off of the bus and waved Charlie over to a huge poster on the bulletin board at the entrance of the school. "Look, basketball tryouts are next week for the boys' and girls' teams. You play basketball, right? So do I. We can be twinsies and both play. Then I can get the girls' basketball team to watch your games, and you can get the boys to watch the girls' games."

"Twinsies?" I looked at Samantha and Ashley and rolled my eyes. *Is there anything this girl doesn't do?*

"Yeah, I play." He looked at the poster to check the dates and times.

I stepped in. "What Charlie meant to say," I looked at Samantha for support, "was that he and I both play. I'll be at tryouts too."

Charlie gave me a strange look. Like he knew I was annoyed, but didn't know what I could possibly be annoyed about.

Samantha shook her head. "Boys can be so stupid," she whispered.

Chapter 43

"MRS. MCGEE, WHERE ARE YOU?" I wandered in through her kitchen, looking for her.

She came out from the laundry room with a basket of towels. "Hello, my sweet girl. Let me give you a big hug and then come sit and have a snack while I fold. There are some mint cookies in the pantry, and you know where the milk is. In fact, I'll have some with you."

I went around the kitchen, gathering up our snack, and started helping her fold the towels. "Mrs. McGee, I think I'm turning into a crazy girlfriend—the kind I swore I would never want to be."

She laughed. "Greta Grace, I don't think you have it in you to turn into a crazy girl, but I'm all ears."

"No, seriously, Mrs. McGee. My blood was boiling today. You probably would have seen steam come out of my ears. You see, Courtney saw a sign for basketball tryouts, and she called Charlie over and said they could be twins by both trying out. But I play basketball. Don't you think he could have at least mentioned that they wouldn't be 'twinsies' because I play too? I mean, really, would it have been that big of a deal?"

Mrs. McGee handed me another towel. "Nobody is ever going to handle things the way you think they should, one hundred percent of the time. The important thing is to talk it out and if they mess up, they apologize; just like if you mess up, you apologize."

"I'm just not sure if he should be apologizing or if I should be, or if it's really Courtney who should be apologizing."

"Hey, you two." Courtney barged into the kitchen. "Greta Grace, did you ask about the Halloween party?"

"No, sorry. It never even crossed my mind."

"Grandma, can we have a Halloween party here? We could set up the basement with orange and black streamers, and everyone can bring sodas and snacks. Is that okay?"

Mrs. McGee smiled at us both. "I don't see why not. I'll leave it up to the two of you to organize."

"Great, then. Greta Grace, the party is on!" Courtney came over and gave me a high five.

· · · · ·

Ashely, Samantha and I decided to be M&Ms. It was a simple costume to put together because Samantha and I wore them last Halloween. Ashley found it online and ordered it in a different color. Anyway, we couldn't think of anything else.

Courtney wanted hers to be a surprise, so we would have to wait until the party to find out. She invited tons of her other friends from our school.

The night of the party, Courtney went around, checking the decorations one more time. "We did a good job, Greta Grace. This place looks awesome."

"Okay, I've got to go. Ashley and Samantha are arriving at my house in two minutes, and it'll take me longer than that to ride my bike home. I'll see you in a bit."

The girls were already at my house. Samantha stuck her head out my bedroom window. "Greta Grace, hurry!"

She and Ashley were already ready. "Sorry, I'm late, but the decorating took longer than we thought. You should see the great decorations Courtney got."

"Okay. Talk while you get dressed." Samantha handed me a green leotard with tights and two huge green circles with M's on them; one for the front of me and the other for the back.

"Okay. Ready. Let's go." We walked by little kids who were already out trick-or-treating. Most of them had better costumes than we did.

Chapter 44

I SWUNG OPEN MRS. MCGEE'S DOOR. "We're here!" Mrs. McGee greeted me with a big hello and a side hug. I was too big for her to get her arms around me.

"You know where the party is, Greta Grace. Off you go." Mrs. McGee let out a laugh. It was perfect. The lights were dim, and our cobwebs were strategically placed.

"Hey, everyone!" I yelled over the music as I got to the bottom of the steps.

A girl dressed in a skimpy black leotard, black tights and cat ears jumped up off a boy's lap and ran over to say hello. "You're here! We did an awesome job, didn't we?"

Just then, I got a better look at the girl. "Courtney?"

"Yes, of course it's me! Hi, Ashley. Hi, Sam."

After getting a glimpse of the boy, I turned to Ashley and Samantha. "Was I seeing things or was she sitting on Charlie's lap?"

"No, you were not seeing things." Ashley placed her hands on her hips. "You better stand up to that girl. No more sitting back and taking it anymore, Greta Grace."

I could hear Mom's voice going through my head. "Sometimes the hardest conversations to have are the most important ones." *But was this really an important one to have, or was I making a stupid big deal out of nothing?*

"But what if I look like a crazy jealous girlfriend?" I looked at the two girls. I just wasn't sure how to handle this one.

"Okay, so if you don't say something, are you going to be okay with her sitting on his lap from now on?" Ashley spoke as if someone had just wronged her and not me. "It's called boundaries, Greta Grace. You've got to set some boundaries."

"Okay. Here it goes. My hands are sweaty. Do you really think I should do this?" They pushed me forward to make sure I went.

"Hey, GG. I like your costume!" Charlie looked up from the can of soda he was trying to open. *Not nearly as exciting as a kitten, I'm sure.*

I have to do this. I asked Charlie, "Hey, can we maybe go outside for a couple of minutes?"

"Yeah, sure." He followed me up the stairs. "What's up?"

I sat down on Mrs. McGee's front steps, looked down at my hands, and then looked up. "Okay, you might think I'm crazy, but I just don't think it's okay to let a girl sit on your lap like Courtney did."

"Oh. You're right. Sorry about that." He gave me a hug, at least as much of a hug as he could around my M&M costume.

"So, we're good?" I wanted to make sure he hadn't just written me off as one of the crazies.

"We're good. Now let's go back and enjoy the party." He smiled and grabbed my hand to walk back inside.

"There you two are! I was looking for you." As we started back downstairs to the party, Courtney ran up and threw her arms around both of us.

But I wasn't done. "Hey, can we talk, Courtney?"

"Sure." Charlie headed back to the party, while Courtney followed me outside. "What's up?"

"I don't know. I just think it's weird that you were sitting on Charlie's knee and flirting with him. Friends don't do that to each other."

"You aren't serious, are you? Oh my gosh, Greta Grace! He may be your boyfriend, but he's allowed to have friends, even friends who are girls. And I don't like him, and I'm not flirting. That's just my personality. I can't change."

"Really? I'm pretty sure you can."

"Oh, my gosh. If it's that big of a deal to you, then fine. I am going to try, but if I forget, you can't get all mad and stuff. I'm not trying to steal your boyfriend. C'mon, let's get back to the party." She opened the door, and I followed her inside.

"How did it go?" Ashley and Samantha both wanted to know.

"With Charlie, I think it went fine. With Courtney, I actually have no idea."

"Okay, everybody, get up and dance *right now*!" Ashley screamed above the music and voices.

Samantha and I laughed at her craziness, but she knew how to get the party going. Everybody got up and danced.

. . . . .

Mom was sitting up waiting when Ashley's dad dropped me off.

"Hey, sweetie. How was your night?" She was sitting at the kitchen table in her robe and slippers, sipping a cup of tea and reading a contract for work.

"It was good, even though it had a really strange beginning." I poured some milk for myself and grabbed a handful of cookies. "The thing is, I like Courtney, but I'm afraid if she doesn't stop flirting with Charlie, he's going to end up liking her instead of me. I mean, it's not right for her to flirt with him when she knows I really like him. Right?"

"No, Greta Grace. Friends don't do that to each other. Maybe you should have a conversation."

"Well, they know how I feel about it because I talked to both of them."

"Good girl, Greta Grace, and what did they say?"

"Charlie got what I was saying. Courtney said she will try, but I can't get mad if she forgets."

"Forgets, hmm. Let's see how that goes before we assume the worst, but I am proud of you. We all know that sometimes the hardest conversations are the most important ones to have."

"I *knew* you would say that!" I laughed as I threw myself on the couch with my cookies. I clicked on the TV. "What are we watching?"

Chapter **45**

COURTNEY CAME RUNNING INTO OUR SCIENCE CLASS just before the bell rang and threw her backpack on a desk. "Hey, you two. How about we practice some basketball tomorrow after school before tryouts the next day? I haven't played since last season."

Charlie quickly agreed. "Sure, I'll play."

"Um, Charlie," I said, "I thought we were going to the library tomorrow after school to study."

"Oh, yeah. We can go after basketball, right?" He looked at me like that would be no big deal.

"I can't. I have to walk home, and I have to be there before dark, so that won't work."

"Okay. Then let's just go to the library another day." Charlie got out the books he needed for class.

I pulled my science book out of my backpack and went and sat in my seat.

What a jerk. What a total jerk!

The teacher taught the lesson, but I had zero idea what it was on because I sat there and kept replaying in my mind the scenario that had just happened. *What a jerk!*

I looked down, and someone was tossing a note on my desk. It was from Casey.

> Are you okay? I could talk to Courtney if you want, or you know I could bust her up or something. Just kidding! Those days are gone. BTW, sorry about that.

I turned toward her, smiled, and shook my head. Wow! How far we had come. Less than a year ago, her notes would have been threatening me.

I wrote back:

> Thanks, but it's okay. No need to talk or bust her up! Haha!

Then I sent the note back her way.

The bell rang, and I got up and walked ahead of everybody to get out of the classroom.

"Hey, GG. Wait up." Charlie called after me.

"Yeah?" I stopped and turned toward him for a minute.

"What's wrong? You seem mad."

"Why would I be mad? I mean, just because we had plans to go to the library, and you decided to play basketball instead. Why in the world would that make me mad?"

"I don't get it. What's the big deal?"

"Exactly, you don't get it, and that's the problem." I walked away and decided to skip taking the bus for today.

Chapter 46

"MRS. MCGEE! ARE YOU HOME?" Her door was locked. *Please be home. Please be home.*

"Hello, my sweet girl." Mrs. McGee opened the door to let me in. "I must have accidentally locked the door after coming in from the grocery store. Lord knows I would never lock you out."

"I'm glad you're home because I think I am going to explode into the next galaxy if I don't get this off of my chest. You see, Charlie and I had planned to go to the library, but then Courtney asked us to play basketball. I said I couldn't, but Charlie said he could, even though he had agreed to go to the library with me. I know Courtney asked both of us and not just him, so I can't be mad at her, but really, don't you think that's pretty thoughtless of him? I know there's the whole 'willingness to see things differently' thing, but I can't just not be mad about this." I took off my shoes and tossed my backpack on the bench by the coat rack.

"Oh my. I wonder what he's thinking? It seems like he really doesn't have a clue what he does to your feelings until after it's done. Maybe you're the first person he has ever really liked, so he doesn't know better, or maybe that's just his way and he's always going to be like that. Either way, you don't have to stick around if it's not working for you."

"I know, but it would be so much easier to walk away if I knew he was a jerk and just not clueless." I let out a big sigh while I sat Rudy on my lap and stroked his back. "I want to come back as Rudy in my next life."

"Hi, Grandma. Hey, Greta Grace." Courtney bounced in and took a seat next to me. "I just saw your boyfriend. I realized I needed some new basketball sneakers because mine are now about two sizes too small, so I had him go to the sporting goods store with me to get some new ones. You know, it's that little store right by school. So, tell me about these tryouts, Greta Grace. What am I in for?"

"Really?" I said and then gave her a look that clearly asked, "You couldn't pick out sneakers on your own?"

"Oh, stop. It's not a big deal. I just wanted someone to come with me, and Casey had to go straight home to babysit. So tell me about tryouts."

Mrs. McGee listened without saying a word, but she kept looking at me to see just how upset I really was.

"I'm not sure," I told her. "They're tryouts. The same as all tryouts. You go, you play, and you either make it or get cut." *Really? She had to ask Charlie to pick out sneakers with her? And he went?*

"Well, no worries about any of this. Just do your best girls and trust that something good will come of it either way. You know, your mom, Courtney, didn't make the cheerleading team in high school. At first she was devastated, but then she decided to try volleyball and she loved every minute of it." We both just looked at her.

I told Courtney, "Hopefully, we'll both make it." Was I disturbed that she asked Charlie to go shopping with her? Yes! Was I hoping that she wouldn't make the team. No!

Just then, a text came in from Charlie.

Hey.

Hey.

What are you doing?

Hanging out with Mrs. McGee and Courtney. You?

Doing homework. Are you coming to play basketball tomorrow after school?

No. I'm going to the library because I have a big test coming up. I'll practice shooting at the hoop in my yard after it. You can practice with me if you want.

This is where I thought he would say that he would go to the library too.

> Oh. Okay. See you tomorrow
> in school.

I looked at my phone and screamed at it. "What? Are you kidding me?"

"Whoa! What is going on?" Courtney looked shocked.

"Listen to this." I read the conversation aloud.

"What's the big deal? Who cares? You go to the library, and he'll go to basketball."

And here I realized the big dilemma. Was I truly being a drama queen who was totally overreacting, or was this guy completely out of sync with reality? Or worse yet, was Courtney up to something, and I just didn't want to believe it?

"Mrs. McGee, what do you think?"

"I say that if you sit in stillness, all your answers are inside of you. Trust yourself. That's what I say."

I knew she was right.

Courtney rolled her eyes. "Oh God, Grandma. Do you make her do all that stuff that you made my mom do? That's so strange. Thank God my mom doesn't make me do it."

Chapter 47

"TIME TO GET BACK TO THE BASICS, GRETA GRACE." I spoke out loud to myself. I pulled out my yoga mat, opened up a meditation app on my phone, lit a candle, closed my eyes, and took some deep breaths.

It was peaceful. It was calming. I cleared my head of all worries and sat quietly. I had no idea how much time had gone by until I heard Mom's voice.

"Greta Grace. I'm home, sweetie. Come on down, I picked up some dinner for us."

I ran down the stairs to greet her.

"Greta Grace, I'm sorry work is taking up so much of my time lately, and we have been eating all this take-out. I am way behind on the laundry, and there aren't any snacks in the pantry, and..."

"Oh my gosh, Mom. Stop. We are fine. I am fine. Actually, I can start doing my own laundry."

She hugged me tight and then put out a plate for each of us, and we divided up the Chinese food. "Where has the time gone, Greta Grace? You are growing up too fast on me."

I loved Chinese food, and it was nice that Mom was so crazy busy, but she still made time to get this for us.

During dinner, I heard my phone ringing upstairs, and I was anxious to see who the missed call was from. Mom's rule was that there was never, ever a good reason to check a phone during meals, so I had to go all through dinner without knowing who called me. As soon as we finished eating and cleaned up everything, I ran upstairs to check.

It was from Charlie. I threw myself down on my bed and called him back.

He picked up on the first ring. "Hey. What's up?"

"Hey there. Well, I just did my homework and ate dinner, and soon I'm going to do laundry." I left out the part about meditating. That just might scare him off.

"So Casey texted me and she, um, she said that you're probably really mad about the basketball thing after school. So I'm going to go to the library with you instead."

I wasn't sure how I felt. I told him, "I don't want you to go because you feel like you have to. I only want you to go if you want to, if you *really* want to; not because you feel bad."

"I do want to go. I swear. I just wasn't thinking because I'm not really a library kind of kid, but I do want to go with you."

"Okay! Then we'll go to the library." *Casey actually had my back.*

Chapter 48

WHEN SAMANTHA AND I PICKED UP COURTNEY for school the next morning, she stormed out of Mrs. McGee's house wearing the tiniest miniskirt I had ever seen and a skin-tight, black long-sleeved T-shirt.

"Are you kidding me?" she demanded.

"What? What are you talking about?" Samantha jumped in quickly.

"Charlie. Are you forcing him to go to the library after school instead of playing basketball?" She rolled her eyes in disgust at me. "I need to practice. I need someone to practice with me."

"Uh, no. But how do you know, and why are you so upset over it?" I looked at Samantha to see if I had missed something.

"I know because I texted him to make sure he was coming. I just think it's stupid." She pulled the door closed hard behind her and walked by us.

"Stupid that he's not playing basketball after school with you or stupid he's going to the library?" I called to her.

"Both. Lighten up, Greta Grace. It wasn't a big deal."

Hmm. Why is she so upset over this?

"I don't know, Courtney," Samantha said. "I think if he was your boyfriend, and the tables were turned, you would be mad too. It's called boundaries, Courtney. People have boundaries!"

Samantha sounded like a mom.

"Whatever! Seems totally stupid to me." Courtney was clearly in a bad mood this morning. Samantha and I let her walk farther ahead so there was a lot of distance between us.

"Hey, GG." Charlie met me with a huge smile as I scooted into our seat on the bus.

Courtney looked at Charlie. "So, you're seriously not going to play after school?" Courtney and Casey pushed into their seats.

"Nah, I'm going to go to the library with GG."

"Whatever." Courtney flung her hair over her shoulder and turned away.

"Hmm. Someone seems a little more annoyed than she should be." Samantha turned and studied Courtney. Thank goodness it was soon time for us to get off of the bus.

I stood next to Samantha and watched Courtney and Casey walk away.

"You know what it is, right? She has really never not gotten her way. This is ruffling her feathers," Samantha said as she shrugged her shoulders.

"You're probably right, but I can't let any of this bother me anymore. He says he likes me, so I'm not going to let Courtney drive me crazy. Plus, I realized she's not going to be here forever. Her parents will want her back in Massachusetts someday. Who knows? Maybe she truly is that nervous about trying out and really wanted to practice with someone."

"Let me guess. This is you practicing how to see things differently, right?" Samantha smiled.

"Yes, it is. I don't know. It just doesn't feel like it's more than that. Anyway, it's better than making myself nuts by holding a grudge for the rest of the day."

"But what happens if while you're trying to see things differently, she swoops in and steals your boyfriend?"

"Then God's got a better plan. You might have to remind me of that, but it is the truth."

"You realize you're the only eighth grader on the face of the planet who would say something like that. You sound like you're a hundred years old. No, actually you sound like you're a thousand years old." Samantha laughed and slammed my locker shut for me.

Well, changing my perception worked out just fine for the day. I wasn't all grumpy about Courtney, and Charlie and I had a great time hanging out at the library together.

Chapter 49

"GRETA GRACE, C'MON. HURRY UP. We have to get to tryouts." Courtney came running up to my locker with her school backpack thrown over one shoulder and her sports backpack thrown over the other.

"Okay. Wish me luck!" I whispered to Samantha and took off to tryouts with Courtney.

"Wow! I had no idea there would be this many people trying out." I sat on the side of the court and tied my sneakers while girls poured out of the locker room.

"We'll be fine." Courtney took a big gulp of water and started bouncing the ball between her legs. "I found a bunch of kids playing who let me play with them, so I think I'm ready."

"Okay. Half of you take a green pinny and the other half take a blue one and line up according to positions.

I'll rotate you in and out." The coach was stern, with nothing friendly about him at all.

Courtney and I grabbed two green pinnies and lined up on the side of the court. "You. Out to the court." He pointed at me.

I closed my eyes. Okay. *God, here it goes. Angels, I'm calling you in to help me do my best. Help my feet be fast and my shots be accurate.*

He placed enough girls on the court for two teams and blew the whistle. "Game on!" He rotated players in and out. Guess who rotated in for my position? Yep. Courtney.

· · · · ·

"Well, do tell, girls! How did the tryouts go?" Mrs. McGee met us at the door.

"Horrible." Courtney threw her basketball sneakers in the hall closet and then made her way into the kitchen, where she grabbed a bottle of water.

"Well, regardless, I am proud of the two of you for putting yourselves out there. You should be proud of that too."

"Whatever." Courtney said as she scrolled through her phone.

"I better get going. Mom probably has dinner waiting." I grabbed my stuff and headed toward the door.

"Where are you going without giving me a hug?" Mrs. McGee came over and hugged me tight.

I felt bad for Courtney, but she already had so much going for her. I knew she would be fine, even if it didn't turn out the way she wanted.

· · · · ·

Mom met me at the gate when I got home. She grabbed me by the hand and dragged me into the house. "Greta Grace! Come, sweetie! I just received an email saying that they have posted the roster for basketball."

"I can't look. You look and tell me the results." I sat down on the couch and closed my eyes. I was excited and nervous at the same time.

"Ahh! Greta Grace, you made it." She threw her arms around me.

I jumped up and ran over to look at the rest of the roster. I scoured the list. "Ugh! Courtney isn't on the list. She's probably going to be really mad. I'm going to go text Charlie, Mikey, Samantha and Ashley to tell them." I would have been happy if Courtney made the team with me. But honestly, I would have been a little upset if she made it without me. I guess you could consider me a work in progress.

"Perfect. You go do that, and I'll order a pizza. That's always a good celebratory dinner."

Chapter 50

THE NEXT MORNING, Samantha arrived right on time, and I, for once, was ready for school. Miracles do happen.

"Okay, I'm not sure if Courtney is upset over the tryout results, so don't say anything about it. I don't want things to be awkward." I made sure Samantha was on board with the plan.

"She's allowed to not be good at something. She'll just have to deal with it, like the rest of us do." Samantha answered. "Seriously, the second Courtney doesn't get her way, her whole world falls apart. She should just get over herself."

"Hey, Court," I said as she walked out of Mrs. McGee's with another super-tight skirt and top on.

"Hey!" She ran up and hugged me. "I'm so happy for you. I knew you would make it."

Samantha gave me a weird look. I knew by now that we were thinking the same thing. Was Courtney seriously that happy for me? I couldn't exactly figure this girl out.

"Who knows? Maybe next year I'll make it." She shrugged her shoulders.

"Next year? I thought you were going back to Massachusetts at the end of the school year." Samantha said what we were both thinking.

"Ever since my grandmother got sick, my parents decided they want to live closer to her so they are looking for houses here in Fairfield. I'll be staying! Isn't that great? I'm so excited. Actually, Samantha, they are looking at a house on your street."

Samantha looked away quickly.

I realized this was the conversation Samantha avoided having with me.

"I actually thought it might be your house, but my mom said it's a foreclosure or some word like that. Whatever it is, the people are selling it because they can't pay for it anymore." Courtney took off to share the news that she was moving to Fairfield with everyone else.

Samantha's eyes welled up with tears.

"Is everything okay?" I asked softly.

She shook her head. "Not at all. She's talking about my house."

Thank you for reading *Greta Grace*. If you've enjoyed reading this book, please leave a review on your favorite review site. It helps me reach more readers who can be inspired by Greta Grace as she navigates her way through school.

Discussion Questions

1. In middle school, no one really wants to be different. It never seems like a good time to "try yourself out" or to "be" instead of trying to conform. Greta Grace shows us what a strong sense of self looks like. One example of this is that she's not afraid to talk about the angels sending her triple digits as signs they are with her. Where in the book do you see other examples of her not being worried about being different?

2. Greta Grace was terrified when Casey was bullying her, yet she didn't want to tell her mom. She knew her mother would go to the school, and she thought that would make things worse. What would you have told Greta Grace to do? What would you have done if you were in her shoes?

3. In Chapter 6 (page 20), Greta Grace's mom says to her, "Greta Grace, you are amazing, strong, loveable, and beautiful with an inner bright light shining that cannot be dimmed. That's who you are.

Not even Casey Cunningham can change that." The truth is, every single one of you is all those things. What stops you from believing that about yourself at times?

4. In Chapter 16 (page 54), Greta Grace walks into Mrs. McGee's hospital room. "'Oh, my gosh,'" I whispered. 'She looks like she is dying.'" This was a very sad moment for Greta Grace because she feared losing Mrs. McGee. Have you ever worried about losing someone?

5. In Chapter 19 (page 64), Greta Grace says, "Mom and Mrs. McGee always said something good comes out of everything. Who would have thought that Charlie and Mikey would be my something good out of something very, very bad?" Greta Grace ended up making some great friends despite a painful situation. Can you think of a time when something good came out of something not so good in your own life?

6. In Chapter 22 (page 73), Greta Grace says, "Something inside me told me I just might need it, and so I listened to that voice." Have you ever had a "gut feeling" about something? What do you think that gut feeling is?

7. In Chapter 28 (page 94), Greta Grace's mom says, "But one day down the road, you'll see that by forgiving, you free yourself, not the person who did something to you. It's kind of like a gift to yourself." What do you think she means by this?

8. In Chapters 31 and 32, Greta Grace has the perfect opportunity to embarrass Casey. On page 106, after Casey tells her she better not say anything to anyone about where she lives, Casey says, "How do I know you won't?" Greta Grace responds, "Because I don't live to ruin people's lives. Nobody cares where you live." On page 107, Ashley thinks Casey should get a taste of her own medicine. But Greta Grace says, "'Okay, all hands in.' I put my fist out. We all bumped fists to make it official. No one would say anything. That's the way I wanted it." What are your thoughts about this?

9. In Chapter 34 (page 114), Greta Grace tells us that a quote from her mom and Mrs. McGee pops into her head. "Don't always believe your thoughts." Sometimes our thoughts can have us believe certain things about ourselves that limit us, or thoughts about someone else that we just decide are true. If you were to stop and question something you believe about yourself or someone else, what would it be?

10. In Chapter 35 (page 116), Greta Grace says, "My circle was small these days since I only hung out with Mikey, Charlie and Ashley, but it was a good circle. I guess it is true when they say quality is much more important than quantity." Have you ever had this experience? Can you have quality and quantity at the same time?

11. In Chapter 36 (page 121), Greta Grace is upset over Courtney coming to live with Mrs. McGee. She tells her mom that "It's weird. She changes everything. It's not going to be fine. It's going to be terrible." Her mom understands but then says, "You get to choose how this whole thing plays out." What do you think she means by that? How do you think you would feel about it or handle it?

12. In Chapter 41 (page 137), Samantha talks about a quote Greta Grace's mom has on the fridge. It says, "When you know better, you do better." What do you think this quote is trying to teach you?

13. In Chapter 44 (page 145), Greta Grace says, "I could hear Mom's voice going through my head. 'Sometimes the hardest conversations to have are the most important ones.'" If you were Greta Grace, do you think you would have had the conversations with Charlie and Courtney or would you have been worried about them being mad at you if you did?

14. In Chapter 45 (page 150), Casey passes Greta Grace a note asking her if she wants her to talk to Courtney. Then in Chapter 47 (page 157), Charlie says that Casey texted him to let him know he probably made Greta Grace mad about the basketball thing after school. Were you surprised Casey offered to help Greta Grace after she was so abrupt with her in Chapter 20. Why do you think she softened up so much?

15. In Chapter 46 (page 155), Mrs. McGee says, "If you sit in stillness, all of your answers are inside of you. Trust yourself." What do you think this means? Do you feel like you trust yourself or do you feel like you go to other people to find out what you should do? In response to Mrs. McGee, Greta Grace pulls out her yoga mat, opens up a meditation app on her phone, lights a candle, closes her eyes, and takes some deep breaths. Have you found a way to calm your own mind? How? If not, do you think it would be helpful if you did?

16. In Chapter 48 (page 160), Greta Grace says, "You're probably right, but I can't let any of this bother me anymore. He says he likes me, so I'm not going to let Courtney drive me crazy. Who knows? Maybe she truly is that nervous about trying out and really wanted to practice with someone." Samantha responds with, "Let me guess. This is you practicing how to see things differently, right?" What are your thoughts about this? Have you ever had to try to see things from a different perspective?

17. In Chapter 49 (page 163), Greta Grace says, "I guess you could consider me a work in progress." What do you think she means by this? Do you agree that we are each a work in progress? (I do!)

18. At the end of the book, Samantha reveals that Courtney's family is buying her house because her family can't pay for it anymore. How does this explain Samantha's actions throughout the book?

19. What do you think is going to happen in the next book?

Acknowledgments

To Patrick O'Reilly... Sorry, Dad, for all those times I rolled my eyes as a teen when you summoned us to "think positively" because we could "do anything we wanted to." It's those same thoughts that got this book to where it is. My teen brain just couldn't agree that you might be right, but forty years later, I am here to thank you! Thank you for always believing and for all those stories you had us write when all we really wanted to do was watch TV. Clearly, you knew what you were doing. Loved you then, love you now, and will love you always!

Mom, Ellen O'Reilly, who will probably cringe that her name is even in print or that she would be publicly thanked. In a normal person's eyes, your nurturing, loving, supportive way isn't even on the same frequency as most. I could only hope that my own kids can turn around one day and say that I was half the mom you are. You are amazing, and I couldn't love you more.

Tom Quinn, behind every good woman (at least, I think I am!) is a great guy! This is where you come in. Through our very many years together, not once did you ask me to delay or give up on an endeavor. Some worked out great, others not so great, but guess what? You were still there supporting, loving and cheering me on every single step of the way. You are incredible, and I feel so blessed. I love you.

Morgan Quinn and Tommy Quinn, my two lovies. My very first editors! How long have we been on this book journey? A long time! Thank you for reading and then re-reading. I'm the luckiest mom on Earth to be able to have the two of you call me "Mom." How in the world did I get so lucky? You are two of my greatest blessings. I love you.

Michele Oricoli, Roisin McAdams, Julie O'Reilly and Barry O'Reilly, at various times, the four of you kept me buying into the idea that maybe I would really get this story into print. You guys believed in my book, its lessons, and what it could do for young people, which was an essential ingredient in bringing this to fruition. Sometimes, I needed you to believe so I could believe. So, thank you. Love you, guys.

Pat, Martin and Brendan O'Reilly, you are not forgotten! I may not have bothered all six siblings incessantly about this book, but I do know for sure how loud you cheer for me and all of us! Love you.

JoAnn Turilli, without a doubt, you have been an empowering part of this journey. You are a constant in my life, and I love you for that and for all that we learn from each other, on every spiritual topic imaginable. Thanks for being one of my greatest cheerleaders!

Not everyone has Soul Sistas, but I do! Sage Osa, Amy DeLardi, Lynn Dolynchuk, Katie O'Grady, Colleen Murphy, and Wendy Martinenas, God sure did know what he was doing when he placed the seven of us in that meeting room way back when. At the time, I thought it would just be a good way to join like-minded people and to learn some laws of the Universe. What I didn't realize is that God/Universe had so much more in store for us. All these years later, we are more Soul Sistas than we ever were. To Lynn, an extra thank you for your help with this book! Thank you for helping me understand what I didn't know, that I needed to know! To you all, I am so grateful for your friendship, your support and your love.

Robin Duncan, my spiritual mentor and friend... When I started listening to and then working with you years ago, I had no idea your teachings would change every part of my life, including being able to get this book done. You are one of the brightest lights that I have ever met. Thank you for every single nugget that you have taught me and for always reminding me of the beauty and bounty of God's love. I couldn't be more grateful and while I would never speak for God, I bet he would like me to thank you too! So, thank you. Love, God! For sure, you are one of his Earth angels!

To Emma Barnum, you are a delightful, smart, beautiful young lady whose feedback was greatly appreciated! Thank you!

To Tara Alemany and Mark Gerber of Emerald Lake Books, for all your guidance and support, your wisdom and dedication, thank you! It has been a great journey!

About the Author

J<small>OANNA</small> O'R<small>EILLY</small> Q<small>UINN</small> can usually be found learning something new to teach teens. As a former middle school teacher, founder of Super Empowered One, and life coach, it is no surprise that her middle-grade fiction book, *Greta Grace*, weaves some teachable moments  into her character's very relatable experiences. Think, middle school... Ahhh!

Through her company, Super Empowered One, Joanna teaches kids how to access their confidence, happiness and power, so they can live their best lives.

Joanna loves writing, the ocean, a good run, and living in Fairfield, Connecticut, with her husband and two kids.

Visit her at superempoweredone.com to learn more about her coaching services and *Greta Grace.*

If you're interested in having Joanna conduct a program for your group or come speak to your students, you can contact her at emeraldlakebooks.com/quinn.

For more great books, please visit us at
emeraldlakebooks.com.

CPSIA information can be obtained
at www.ICGtesting.com
Printed in the USA
BVHW071831140921
616731BV00005B/142

9 781945 847448